Order Out of Chaos

By

Gino Gianoli

This book is a work of fiction. Places, events, and situations in this story are purely fictional. Any resemblance to actual persons, living or dead, is coincidental.

© 2002 by Gino Gianoli. All rights reserved.

No part of this book may be reproduced, stored in a retrieval system, or transmitted by any means, electronic, mechanical, photocopying, recording, or otherwise, without written permission from the author.

ISBN: 1-4033-9313-3 (e-book)
ISBN: 1-4033-9314-1 (Paperback)
ISBN: 1-4033-9315-X (Hardcover)

This book is printed on acid free paper.

1stBooks - rev. 12/26/02

"Blessed is He who has crucified the world, and not allowed the world to crucify him"

Aleister Crowley

Order Out of Chaos

A long, long time ago Man dedicated a day to worship the Sun. It was called the day of Sun-Worship, or Sun Day. And so it was that, on the sixth day of the sixth month, Timothy Moone awoke from a dream of blanks to a reality of blurs and found himself lying, face down, on the shores of some beach. He slow and painfully tried to get on his feet, but only managed to get to his knees as the warm blue waters seemed to be taunting him from behind. When he tried to look up he was blinded by the burning rays of the sun. With a deep breath he took a long and confused look around trying to focus on the landscape which he recognized immediately: Miami Beach; then the focus was on himself: his appearance. This one was trickier than the first one. *What had happened to him?* And as soon as he saw all those bruises and scars and bumps and dirt and dried blood spread throughout his legs, his bared torso, arms, shoulders - undoubtedly on his face and back as well-, his body imploded with a lethargic ache sending piercing and severe pains, from his dirty and wrinkled toes, through his legs and crotch, to every tip of his unique blue hair. There was a drought in his mouth, an uprising in his stomach, and a dangerous fog in the memory highways of his mind for he didn't seem to remember how, and why or even *when* he'd gotten there. In fact, he didn't remember anything…anything except for the image of a woman, in a white terry cloth robe, black hair falling, black eyes staring at the identical blueness of the ocean and the sky from the high terrace: He remembered Lara.

It was hot and it was Sunday; an unusual Sunday.

At the bus station at the Mall of the Americas, or as she would say: *"Mall of no Americans"* -meant as a resentful remark at the fact that the city of Miami lacked just that: Americans, English-speaking Americans that is-, Lara Walker hopped on the Greyhound bound for Atlanta: A destination not of her particular choosing but forced upon due to her current situational fuck-up. There, she'd contact Eddie, her cousin -her only known relative as far as she was concerned-, and try to figure out what step to take next. Her mind was over-thinking, over-analyzing, over-projecting. Her eyes examined with extreme prejudice everyone boarding the bus, approaching and passing her seat. Her heart pumped fear into her veins and regret into her brain. The engine started and the door shut.

And like a fugitive on the run, for that is exactly what she'd been for the weeks now. She didn't relax until the bus was well off on I-95 northbound leaving Miami far behind. Then she let off a painful sigh but kept a tight grip on the black leather suitcase that rested on her knees. She stared at it for about twenty seconds; in those twenty seconds her expression shifted from contempt to resignation to hopeful; then proceeded to sort-of caress it with both hands, like nurturing a baby or a puppy.

Then she closed her eyes and rested her head back, but never slept.

To be an artist one must know how to suffer. One must need and even desire to suffer. One must welcome pain. Not the physical but the emotional, the mental and spiritual pain. And it is this sort of pain the artist's everlasting and everflowing source of inspiration, or as they'd call it now, creativity. An artist must provide for his fellow men a kind of beyond-ness, depth-ness, a fourth and fifth dimension to their limited perception of reality, if there's such a thing; reality. But this was not a statement pronounced, or a declaration believed, or a thought meditated; this was a dream dreamed. And this dream was dreamed by Timothy Moone.

Why must a woman feel more guilt than a man? That question lingered in vain in Lara Walker's head for she didn't feel anymore more guilt than Robin Hood and because she also knew the answer. To her it was more like a philosophical question more than anything for she was always a self-provocateur of the mind in its purest and most natural way; she couldn't help it, she was the quintessential modern day rationalist, with a fascination for Nietzsche, a love for Freud, and a fixation on Descartes.

By the expression of her face it was hard to tell whether she was still thinking about the question at hand or the one person she left behind: Timothy, or maybe feeling guilty for doing so. But if one kept looking a little while longer at that facial expression, it wouldn't be so crazy to think that there was a faint trace of fear in there. But if fear is the looking forward towards what will or may happen and guilt the exact opposite: the looking backward to what one has done, then Lara Walker chose not to look at any particular direction for she had learnt not to feel guilt and how to control and balance fear; essential requirements in her line of work.

Timothy Moone always started but never finished. His enthusiasm for anything would always fade before he could reach the end. He couldn't help it, and he was aware of this. God knew he tried, time and again. And this was one of the reasons why he esteemed himself low. His fear of failure was too overwhelming, too soon, especially for a young man, that couldn't be what he wanted. But he didn't really know what failure was, or of what kind of failure he was so terrified from, and many times in the dark hidden rooms in the basement of his mind, he knew that being an artist, or calling one's self an artist, gives one room to fail and be accepted by itself. And although these thoughts and worries never gave him a genuine peace of mind, he was a fairly happy man. He wasn't a sad one for one thing, on the contrary he was alive and full of plans and strange dreams. But even on those bright days of hope and endless possibilities, that ghost, that chain attached to his feet, that weigh wrapped around his waist, that shadow lurking right around the corner of his soul, would creep up on him, uninvited, unwelcomed, unattended. But never ignored.

The abstract thought of failure was etched in his infantile brain by his father; a good-hearted and well-intentioned man that didn't want history repeating itself, again. He himself ended like his father: working shitty jobs, many jobs but never earning enough, living a decent life but on a day-to-day basis. Timothy had to have a better life. He had to have more. And with this creed in his heart and a relentless determination in his mind, he gave young Timothy the few opportunities he never had along with the many demons that afflicted him. His mother on the other hand, never asked much of her son. She was quite content that her Timmy was a well-mannered boy, never got into too much trouble, did well in school and college, and saw life sort of as she did: Simple. What has to happen will happen regardless what one say or does, or doesn't say or doesn't do. We're not as complicated as we think we are. Nothing really is.

These were the hands that shaped Timothy Moone.

And so it was an unusual Sunday morning for the simple fact that on Sundays by the time Timothy Moone regained consciousness, the beaches of South Beach were invaded, stormed and taken by clusters of Bridge Crawlers -a term also used by Lara Walker to amuse herself. But not that Sunday. One could easily say that they were fairly empty, fairly clean and spacious, the white sand seemed whiter than ever and the baby-blue ocean merged seemlessly with the sky at the horizon. And the breeze was warm but refreshing, it felt pure, it felt as if the more he breathed, the deeper the cleansing. And with his aching and beaten body he started walking. Suddenly he thought of Lima. It was the second memory he managed to rescue, to recover from that black hole in his mind. And when he thought of Lima, his second memory, he again thought of Lara, his first. It was there where he first met her. But he didn't push for more, he knew more memories would arrive in due time.

He kept walking south -whether he was aware or not we'll never know- holding his pants up until he reached the pier. There he managed to crawl underneath the boardwalk trying to balance himself on those dark, mossy and slippery rocks until he sat on one of them. He felt something burning in his forehead. His fingers reached for the source of that searing sensation; it felt round, half scab, half flesh. Then, his battered legs, still bearing open wounds, bursted with a burning sensation that turned into an severe itch as they made contact with the ocean waters; but, after they being submerged for a while, a sort of cleansing followed the burning itch, a sensation so relaxing and so invigorating that his body made a sudden and involuntary jump into the water.

Underwater he thought of it all a dream: A light blue liquid reality surrounding him, where no sounds but the deep-tones of his heartbeats were heard and felt; he let himself go, stretching his arms open as if he was waiting for that ever-longed embrace that never comes; his body slowly falling, or maybe drifting sideways, or floating upwards. Soon he would wake up to his regular life, his real life; but how long had he been dreaming? When would he finally wake up? Why is this pain so real? And as the lack of oxygen made him realized that he was in fact awake and underwater, he began to swim upwards in such a chaotic and desperate manner that the water rushed through his nostrils and mouth right before he emerged to take a long and deep breath of air. After his heartbeat stopped pounding and his breathing regained its normal pace, he had then to swim a considerable stretch back to the pier since he had drifted quite a distance.

From where he sat he could see Fisher Island. The water was calmed and warm as usual in this unusual Sunday and every now and then the ripples -that were too big to be ripples- or waves -that were too small to be considered waves- would crash on the rocks where he sat curled and wet, observing and reflecting. The waves -or ripples- were arriving faster and larger now as more and more yachts and boats glided by. Sitting there, contemplating those arrogant peach condos, he remembered that in order to get there one must take the ferry, but to get on the ferry one must be a resident or guest of a resident. He didn't think he'd ever been there. Or had he? There was a faint memory of a house, a large house; an office carved out of wood, dark reddish wood; and thick smoke.

The Bridge Crawlers. This was another term used frequently by Lara Walker to depict the people that would come to South Beach on the weekends, especially on usual Sundays, that came from everywhere outside Miami Beach. The Beach, as the locals would call it, being an island is connected to main land Miami by a series of bridges or Causeways. If you were on the other side of the bridge, you were considered, hopefully only by Lara, a Crawler.

She was in fact very well versed in the art of euphemism. She'd swear on her life that she'd only come up with these names out of sheer fun and were not ill intended or out of general dislike, as some might have suggested, of an overwhelming mix of races and cultures this city adopted. She'd also swear that what lay stashed in the leather suitcase was all hers because she somehow deserved it…because she had the merit and the right to earn it, take it and hopefully get rid of it for a nice price, and then disappear permanently. She really fucked up this time one side of her conscience said. Ok, ok no problems here, only solutions, the other side replied.

Six hours later, driving through Gainsville, Lara felt the urge to take another peek inside the suitcase. She'd never seen so much of it before and if it was what Timothy said it was, then it should be worth more than…anything she'd ever had, or all the things she'd ever had put together. She felt the itch: a line of ants marching through her nape up and into her brain; an acupuncture of curiosity and impatience -the former a hereditary trait, the latter a flaw that in her profession required be suppressed and erased-, a rising of terror and euphoria; and this cocktail of sensations must have had the obligatory splash of hazard and that is why she checked for her gun under her arm: A device that had become throughout time an extension of her arm.

By three o' clock the sun was irate. One could feel the anger of *Ra*, the fury of *Inti*; the God of fire was furious. It seemed as if someone or something had done him wrong, and since he wasn't sure who, and no one was willing to talk, he would make everyone pay. *Burn you insignificant beings, you ants, you bugs, you moths, burn you roaches!*

Timothy Moone heard the sun say this and other things that would only make us hotter.

Timothy Moone the artist was a poet, but not even the lamest prose dared walk through that scorching head of his. He didn't want to complain about the weather, but he had to. He had to damn the damned heat for it was suffocating him; it felt like a noose around his neck, like a mosquito in his ear, it was a bee sting in his tongue, and it weigh like an invincible sack with tons of nothingness on his back. He had started walking from 1st street with high hopes of remembering more about anything, so by the time he got to 15th and Collins Avenue he was as red as a beet and as tire as a bandit's horse with no clear idea where he was going, but northbound. He stopped; he wanted to cry, no!, he wanted to remember. So he just stood there, hopeless, with his breath as dry as paper; his thoughts: sweaty, his disposition: burnt, his desire: bent, and his thinking: slow.

He managed to lift his head up and face the white, tall and trendy looking building ahead of him. Inadvertedly he started getting closer. It was a hotel. The Lowes to be exact. And right there and then another memory managed to swim back in what was now an almost dried lake in his head.

Tell me with whom you go about, and I'll tell you who you are. It was Lara Walker's favorite axiom. To her, Mankind never got so close to the truth as the moment that thought was thought of. She also knew it in Spanish and Italian. She had a thing for languages, she was fluent in four and currently learning her fifth. And if one would ask which one was her favorite; without a second lost pondering, for she didn't have to think this one, before one could even finish asking, she'd shout: *Ma certo il Italiano!*

But not only did she speak, write and think in different languages, but she knew the right usage of such; she was careful with her words, her vocabulary in all those languages was rich and ample. Some appreciated this virtue, others thought of it as pretentious. In any case, she didn't give a flying fuck -she also knew a wide array of profanity- what others thought of her nor their opinions about anything, except when working of course. Lara Walker knew who she was and where she was going. Now she was going to Atlanta escaping from Miami. She never had problems when traveling, she was used to that, her job required of her to be constantly on the move, different cities, different countries, different continents, different times, languages, food, clothing…She welcomed change. Even when it was forced upon her.

Order Out of Chaos

Did she get away with it? Did she? She wouldn't know until later, much later. She wondered how long would she had to stay in Atlanta, she guessed that depended on Eddie, her cousin. She had been on the run for three weeks now, jumping from place to place until finally she thought of Eddie; and after talking to Eddie she thought of peaches.

Eddie was eight and Lara twelve when they last saw each other. Did she still remember how he looked? They had a close relationship as kids: Three times a week their mothers would get together and they'd play, run around, watch movies, share candy, cross-dress, swim and go to the park together; and be involved in other innocent activities such as hide behind the couch and touch each other's genitals with the occasional and exciting lick and kiss.

All that lasted until Lara's folks divorced. Her mother, Beatrice Eleine Caroll, better known as Betty, moved with Lara down to Miami while her father, Randy Walker, moved to Chicago. Obviously they got as far from each other as they geographically could within the country. The sporadic fatherly visits and talks diminished from the frail to a complete break of the relationship. And one day she never heard from him again.

Her skeptic and cynic characteristics were being outlined by then. Armed with an autodidactic passion, Lara always seemed hungry to learn, her favorite word became Why?, she wanted to know, to find out. As she learnt Spanish by the end of her first year in her new city, she also learnt that her mother had become an alcoholic. But *When? How? Mom!* She knew then, at age thirteen, what she didn't want to be.

As she sat there, northbound, watching through the window the flatness and boring landscape of Florida, she felt happy about herself, even when she knew she was being hunted.

The last time she saw her cousin Eddie was when she was twelve that's correct, but the last time she heard about him was much later, perhaps she was nineteen or twenty when she had gone to her mother's house, by then she lived by herself with a roommate, on a Sunday just like this one to visit and spend the day with her, more out of moral obligation than real desire to be there; by that time what she felt for her mother was a love that had transformed into pity and disappointment. There's nothing worse than disappointment Lara would always say.

That day, her mother was on the phone with her sister Marlene, Eddie's mother, who was a sea of tears. She had something terrible to tell her, she was so ashamed and distressed by it. Betty, Lara's mother, immediately walked to the bathroom, opened the cabinet and fished out a couple of pills that went down her throat without the help of any liquids. By this time Betty had traded alcohol for pills. Lara pretended not to see and walked to the kitchen to fix herself something to eat.

Aunt Marlene was hysterical. What had happened was that little Eddie -already sixteen- had been arrested for possession of Marijuana. Of course neither Lara nor Betty thought of it as a huge deal but Saint aunt Marlene did. She was -in her own words- Emotionally destroyed by such realization, her poor little Eddie, her immaculate and only son, had gone astray. The Devil had somehow managed to sneak into her holy sanctuary of a home and chosen little Eddie to be done harm upon. Now her son was a drug addict! it's that Devil's Plant! that has taken ahold of poor Eddie's soul; he'd definitely need some spiritual counseling by none other than Pastor Pete from the church of 'The Chosen Few', which coincidentally enough happens to be right across her home, and only two blocks away from 'The Church of the Immaculate Heart Of Jesus Christ', which oddly enough is also two blocks away from 'The Church Of The New Alliance Of The Sacred Heart Of Jesus Christ', which is not to be confused with 'The Church Of The New Allies Of The Bleeding Heart Of Jesus Christ', which is farther away and their pastor is not as handsome.

In any case, Eddie, thanks to endless nights in vigil and group praying and amen saying, got away with a slap on the wrist by some red-neck judge that had too much to drink the night before. A few community hours will do the boy some good, won't it. After all, the 'possession' consisted in an outrageous half a joint. Well let's thank God and his son Jesus, for saving little poor Eddie from the claws of the Devil's Plant, Praise the lord.

That was a little more than ten years ago. Right now she was hoping, no!, she was counting that her lovely cousin, who was once possessed by the Devil's Plant, would have moved onto bigger things now, and met bigger people, for what she was taking to Atlanta was no half a joint, not a thousand joints, not even marijuana, no, no. The precious cargo she had sitting on her lap since the bus took off from the Mall of no Americans, was no Devil's Plant, hell! the Devil himself would sell his soul for this. This wasn't heroin, no…this was the Breakfast of Gods: Cocaine in its next evolution; ten time as potent, a hundred times as addictive, a thousand times as sweet and a million times its price, created for a sole purpose: to consume the weak and feed the strong. And she carried, in that leather suitcase, eleven full kilos of it. Praise the lord, Eddie!

It was towards that hotel, towards that white, tall, Art Deco structure that his senses pointed to. Yes, blury memories floated by, certain scents came and went and puzzling voices were heard in his head. As he stood on the sidewalk staring at the main entrance where cars were pulling over and taking off, Valets running around like flies over shit, he also remembered that the woman in the white robe had been with him in there. He looked to the highest window, and another series of images flashed back...Was she taking a shower? no, a bath; yes definitely a bath, where he eventually joined her and even though he wasn't one hundred percent sure of it, he was certain of a conversation with her; it was a luxurious bathroom. This had to be it. The more he looked up the more memories stirred inside his brain; after a few minutes the foam bath image had, in fact, taken place...yeah, he remembered...they were sitting facing each other, their bodies submerged in peach scented foam, their slippery legs rubbing, their wandering hands wandering...

Then he was hungry and tired. He was famished and tired. No one knew exactly how long he'd been without a bite of anything; but thirst, never outwitted, rapidly protested and positioned itself as his main priority. Then he was thirsty and tired.

The comings and goings of half naked hotel guests helped our friend reach the main pool without being noticed by hotel personnel, and if he was noticed, he was definitely ignored; there he found a water fountain waiting for him. He drank the cold water calmly and in small dosages; pouring some on his still burning wound in his forehead. The reason why he drank so slow was that he'd heard, as a kid, a story about a man who suddenly found himself stranded in the middle of the desert. Many days passed and many nights passed without finding any water, he walked through the dried dunes and under a scorching sun -similar to this one he thought- for many more days, until finally he reached an oasis where drinkable water was abundant. He rushed to it and began drinking uncontrollably fast without even stopping to breathe, he drank so much so fast that his esophagus and stomach contracted with such force that killed him. He'd heard that story once and never forgot it. Whether true or not, he drank slowly, stopping every few seconds to breathe, take a look around and then continue.

Under a palm tree he meditated -something that he also remembered he knew how to do and used to do often- as the angry old sun got tired of slashing us with his whip of heat, and as it sank behind the by now not-so-baby-blue ocean, it murmured something about humidity. If the sun had an ally it was humidity, if hell did exist, humidity would be the Devil's breath. So once King Sun decided to go punish some other people in some other continent, humidity was instructed to keep reminding us what we're made out of.

And after all that water he drank, Timothy really at that point was made out of water. Water he perspired through his once sand-clogged pores.

There's nothing more exasperating than trying to get out of the state of Florida by bus. At one point it seems frightening endless, frightening long, frightening straight, and definitely frightening flat. After so many hours of flatness one could easily doubt the roundness of the world.

Lara Walker wasn't of the kind to regret, but in this occasion, in this situational context, not bringing a book or a magazine at least, was enough reason to pull one's hair out one by one and really, really re-evaluate one's preparedness skills. But also Lara wasn't of the kind to dwell in her own misery for too long, she'd swallow the bitter pill and draw a satisfied smile on her beautiful face.

Beautiful indeed. Yes she was. Beautiful for her inviting simplicity that'd make one feel at ease, not threatened nor intimidated but heard and understood. Her black eyes, though big, penetrating and round, felt warm and inquisitive in a childish manner. Her long straight black hair shrouded her with mysticism more than mystery. And those thin red lips that curl like a tiny rose, could stretched from cheek to cheek rearranging her porcelain face into a thousand undetermined and undecipherable expressions. Expressions that at an early age she learned to use in a variety of ways, for different occasions and ulterior motives.

As mentioned before, guilt -that greedy damsel that now a days can be seen waltzing and munching on most third world catholic countries- was something that she learned to control and defuse. And that virtue, that asset, made her eligible -at an early age- to be one of The Order's chosen assassins.

As the bus rode through some nameless red-neck town, she closed her eyes and thought of Timothy and wondered what would one feel when one dies? And although she'd seen many people go to the other side in front of her eyes, indeed because of her, she had never really given it much thought. Once again, guilt defused, great asset. After Timothy and death she thought of Lima.

Lima was to Lara the most ambiguous city in the world, it could mean something one minute and something else the next. By meaning she referred to the way the city makes one feel at a particular moment. Sometimes it was alive, bustling with hopes and dreams, then gloomy, sad and disappointed -there's nothing worse than disappointment-. The next day it was clean and the people would stand tall and proud, then, once again dirty, polluted, overpopulated and corrupted in open air. Lima the City of Kings one day, Lima the Ugly the next.

Nighttime in South Beach is chaotic, dangerous, exciting and promising. Each of these adjectives is to some extent the equivalent of fun depending on one's taste. But Timothy Moone didn't think about this, he was still hungry, tired and lost. He knew he had to find something to eat soon before his stomach started eating the other organs, he knew he had to find a place to rest for he had been walking for hours on end. What he didn't know was that by the time he'd think there was no hope, he would be re-introduced to one of the two sides of his previous life.

It's funny how as soon as one crosses the imaginary state line of Florida into Georgia, the landscape doesn't seem so flat anymore. Lara couldn't sleep. She could think and plan and remember and project her self, but goddamnit she couldn't sleep.

He walked through dirty and smelly alleys as it started to get dark. The hidden dirty and smelly backs to the colorful and musical inviting fronts. He needed something to eat, anything. He'd seen some homeless people earlier, scavenging and swimming in the dumpsters. There was not another choice. Either he killed hunger or hunger killed him. Then, there it was, the scent…that unforgettable scent, that unique and unmistakable scent…sauted Foie Gras! he said outloud. His favorite. He followed the invisible trace. He traced the invisible streak with his nose. Sir? He closed his eyes and thought of himself one of those cartoons that floated as they followed the scent of food. Sir? Sir? He opened his eyes and saw a black young man in a restaurant uniform. Mr.Tim Sir? Mr.Tim? He stood there and tried to retake the scent, but now it was everywhere, it was coming from the door behind that young black man. Oh shit man! it's…oh my god! Mr. Tim what the…The young black man ran inside leaving the trashbag he was supposed to throw in the dumpster on the floor. Soon everyone from the restaurant would run back to the alley to see what they could not believe.

Now that sleeping was an improbability rapidly turning into an impossibility, she finally thought of The Order. Actually she'd never stopped thinking about it. How could she? Just the name itself divides her life in two uneven parts: First the life of a young precocious girl trying to cope with her harsh familiar reality to later suppress it and deny it; the second half, the life of a young and apt woman with enough wit to come to terms with herself and shed the old skin to become acknowledged and admired with such adjectives as stealthy and lethal by the other members of the new family that had adopted and given her the recognition she so desperately needed. More than a organization, more than a name, The Order had been and still was an idea, as abstract as freedom, as ancient as chaos, as infinite as numbers; as relevant to her as her own existence. So why? Why did she take the suitcase from Timothy? If she hadn't they'd be after him instead.

She couldn't stop thinking about it. About the suitcase, Timothy and them. As long as she was working for them it meant security, physical and financial. But not anymore. The thought, the idea of The Order had another connotation now, one that it always had, the other side of the coin sort of speak. Now that idea meant retribution. Just like the God of the Old Testament: An eye for an eye. But they were known to take it a little further than that. That's exactly what she did for them. Most of the time she'd get send to take care people that she knew nothing about, these were known as Targets and she thought of them as just that; but there were times when she had to take care of the ones whom had dared to turn on them, people whom perhaps she knew, these were a little tougher but she would go through. Guilt and fear must be defused. And she felt nervous. Nervous and scared. Scared and terrified. Terrified and paralyzed. She hadn't felt this kind of dread since the days when she slowly realized that her father didn't want anything to do with her. But this dread, this heightened fear was a bit different, for beyond their ubiquitous ethereal and material presence, it was the overwhelming idea of them that was breathing over, with and for her.

But before Lara Walker could reach Atlanta and Timothy Moone find out what really happened to him, one must return to those ever fugitive and never precise points in time where everything -and anything- related -or unrelated- to this story, started, or at least make a bonafide attempt at it. And although one also ought to stick to the linear nature of our reality, to the logical continuum of a story line, this one didn't, this one doesn't, this one won't. For it continues stubbornly, it keeps unfolding inwards and outwards and is complete and madly in love with its quantum leaps.

So, until we find a way to sort these pieces of narrative out, in a boring but required, chronological manner, we shall attempt to tell this story as it unfolds, or as it happened to the people involved in it. We shall try to achieve order out of chaos.

Bonn, Germany

"...and thus, Political Asylum should be regarded as the most precious gem of the Diplomatic System, and though it must be secured and protected, it must also be continuously brushed and polished to guarantee its sheltering shine to all its eligible petitioners". With this statement Aesma Daeva closed his speech to the Council of Thirteen, and the lower members of The Order.

As he stepped down from the podium he walked into a series of handshakes and pats on the backs from colleagues and senior members; praise and admiration floated among the roar of applause his speech had generated from the board. For this meeting, in addition the usual thirteen high members of the Council, the presence of the other twenty sub-members, who stood in awe watching the great man leave the board room, was required. Immediately following his departure from the room, the votes were cast in favor of a seemingly insignificant change in the international diplomatic community regarding certain political asylum statutes. And as any decision originated, debated, and agreed upon the members of this Council, it would become international law.

Within the warm and pleasurable confines of the black Mercedez Benz limousine, he thought about Vladimir's expression as soon as he'd hear the good news. Now that he was going to be granted political asylum, amid the many charges of extortion, corruption, money laundering and creation of paramilitary death squads while in the presidency, they, or rather he, could now begin sketching the plan of Vladimir's return to power in his country; but for now they had to wait and see who would become the next president.

There were two runners up: The first, a one Jose Carlos Echevarria was leading the polls. He promised a radical change in internal policy, specifically getting rid of all the corrupted government officials. He wasn't linked to any of the traditional political parties, an independent with ties to no one, therefore too hard to control or influence, a potential problem. The second, a one Ignacio Valverde, a poor bastard that not even he knew how he got as far as he did. Corruptible, inexperienced and greedy, he was definitely the choice to occupy the presidency, the one who would pave the way for Vladimir's return.

Already by this time Aesma Daeva and the Council of Thirteen had placed specific people in strategic positions around the world, whether it be government, banks, military, even pharmaceutical and corporate. In any influential entity, if the head of the organization wasn't placed by the Council, the second head was; sometimes directly, many times indirectly.

Vladimir was one of his favorite pupils, he showed great potential for leadership. He had spread his influence as fast and deep as no other leader had in his country, but one oversight, and that's all it takes, brought everything down for him. But the damage shall be repaired.

No one knows the story of Aesma Daeva. No one knew where he came from and most people didn't even even know his name and that ones who *had* heard it, didn't know what he looked like; whether he was old or young, real or a myth. The few that had seen him, like Vladimir, didn't know how old was he or in what country he was born, whether he had parents, or children, a wife, no wife. Nothing.

Of course many stories started to boil up to make up for the lack of information. Some said he had many wives and lived in Iceland in a secluded mansion from where he conducted his meetings; others said that he had sold his soul to the Devil and had a powerful influence on the powerful and influential. And others even said that *he* was the Devil himself, who ruled the world, the power behind the throne. The fact was that only a chosen few had seen him and even them didn't know for certain that he was Aesma Daeva head of the Council of Thirteen. So perhaps he was the Devil after all.

As the Mercedez glided through the frozen streets of *Konrad Adenahuer Platz,* a voice at the other end of the line informed him of the latest news from Lima. First, what the people were saying and what the media knew about Vladimir Guzman's escape and unknown whereabouts; next, the latest opinion polls for the upcoming presidential elections: Jose Carlos Echevarria was leading them by a ten point margin to Ignacio Valverde. Although expected, they weren't good news, but a third revelation would really make him think and remember: the daughter of Jose Carlos Echevarria, a one Patricia Echevarria, happened to be a member of The Order. She was the main contact in Lima in charge of providing up-to-the-minute information about a chosen Target. He'd had to think this one through.

Everyone has a price. Vladimir Guzman believed in this modern truth with all his heart. To him there was a logical explanation for it: If he, when in the presidency, the most powerful man in his country, the one man that in one way or the other affected everybody's life; if he, who at the snap of the finger could have almost anything he'd desired, if he, who had it all had a price, therefore anyone who had less, which would be the rest of the country, definitely *had* to have a price. He was aware the price could mean money to some, power to others, fame or even sex to many. Everyone has a price because everyone wants something, everyone wants more. Human desire is everlasting, evergrowing and will never be satisfied, Vladimir once said this to him; and he agreed. He also knew that Vladimir's price was power. He had everything else. In his payroll while in the presidency, one could have found such prominent names and titles, that more than awe and disappointment, would cause disgust and envy. Such people included the Mayor of Lima, of course, and at least fifteen other Mayors and Governors around the country, selected Congress Men and Senators, Military officials, CEO's and Media Moguls, Sport Celebrities and even the Archbishop. With a net as extensive and influential: *Why the hell did he have to escape the country?*

Aesma Daeva knew why.

Somehow a document; legal in its nature, precise in its accusation, concise in its content and devastating in its charges, ended up in the Media, specifically Channel Four; one of the few that were not part of Vladimir's 'League of Friends'. And thus, that twenty page document was enough to start one of the biggest political scandals in the history of the country. What the Peruvian people didn't realize was that in a matter of four years they would witness another scandal involving yet another president that would put this one to shame; for not only they'd be able to read about it, but they'd actually be able to watch the crime, repeatedly, on all TV stations in the comfort of their living rooms.

The limousine finally got on the Autobahn to get into an even heavier traffic. But he was unfazed by this. The unification and free commerce of the European nations had transformed Germany's Autobahns into the main arteries of European trade; arteries that were being clogged and atrophied by an ever increasing number of multinational trucks and trailers. Dutch trucks coming, French trucks going, Belgium trucks in front, Italian trucks behind…He watched and understood. He understood and contemplated. He contemplated and smiled, for it was all his creation: The unification of territories, even as an abstract thought; disappearance of demarcation and borders when it came to trade; the uniformation of the currency, and soon that of people's mentalities. And to think that not so long ago, many thought this, insane, outrageous, improbable. Well, he had to smile again.

Lima, Peru

When Senator Anais Echevarria arrived to her office in Congress that early morning of early spring, she'd never thought in a thousand years that in her mail, inside that manila envelope, there was a videocassette that would not only bring her into the spotlight and change her life, at least her political life, forever, but it would unleash a Presidential resignation and prosecution, motivate a mass military expelling and demoting, force many coworkers and fellow senators to step down and others to seek refuge in their parliamentary immunity, but uncork the biggest, largest and deepest corruption scandal in Peruvian history since the discovery and publishing of the documents that forced ex-President Vladimir Guzman out of office four years ago.

But Anais had no idea just yet. That morning she got out of bed tired and tense, she hadn't been able to sleep all through the night. Was her daughter in trouble? The day before she had received an e-mail in her office computer that notified her of the clandestine activities of her daughter Patty. Illegal activities that had international links to underground organizations involved among other things, sabotage and drug and arms trafficking. Nonsense!

Outrageous! she thought. She was only twentyfive years old and attending her last year in law school. Soon she'd take the bar exam, pass it and become a successful lawyer and future senator, and maybe, who knows, President. So that was certainly a shameless accusation, or some jealous person playing a prank on her, or them...yes that's it. Someone jealous of a successful woman in a macho society with an equally successful daughter with the clear potential to continue her mother's legacy in her father's memory.

After the maid cleared the breakfast table, she headed for her daughter's old room. It still looked and smelled the same as when she left. Same comforters, same drawings, same scent of childhood. A scent she hadn't smelled in a long time. And that scent reminded her of another forgotten scent: Her husband's. Four years had slowly crawled by. Four years since he left to the store that one morning and never came back. Four years since the funeral. Four years since the accusations and dubious convictions. Four years without 'i love you's' or 'good night's'. She composed herself before she broke down, she had to go.

The chauffeur stopped at a red light on *Avenida Colonial* on their way to Congress; Anais stared out the tinted window in the back seat and saw the same

Order Out of Chaos

streets with different eyes, the real reality of the capital city; its current state of misery and desperation, cynicism, and hopelessness: kids that in first world countries, this early in the morning, would be either in school playing with crayons and clay or at home watching television, were there begging for mercy and some change; adolescents with lost looks in their eyes waiting for something to happen and young adults with hopeless dreams were selling candies and single-cigarettes instead of preparing for the future. All this she saw in the foreground, for as a backdrop the sky seemed as dark and dirty as the faces of the kids staring at that big black car driving by, wherein she comfortably sat inside.

Her soul was as overcast as the sky above. She wanted to cry and the sky wanted to rain; but none could. The trembling liquid in her eyes lasted a few seconds longer than the weak drizzle that could've been an illusion if it wasn't for the tiny drops on the windshield. God Jose Carlos, did you really think you could've change this country? I guess no one will ever know right?

Gino Gianoli

Paris, France

Aesma Daeva always, since early in his youth, liked to sit and contemplate the intricate grandiosity of the Cathedral of Notre Dame; it's dark connotations from even darker times fascinated and inspired him.

That cold and misty morning, he thought about the people involved in its construction; the pain, the work, the infinite years, the master minds…those 13th century master minds behind that magnificent expression of devotion, those rose windows, those richly carved portals; but it was one, the entrance, that called his attention more than anything, especially the center doorway depicting his favorite biblical story: The last judgment.

There, on the bench, he would light a cigarette and with every drag, he would focus on a specific area of the facade. The relaxed reverberation of the Seine did nothing but enhanced the enjoyment of silent observation and beauty appreciation. Beautiful indeed. And majestic as well; Napoleon himself thought of no better place to be crown emperor. Or was it Josephine who had the fine taste?

After the purifying conscious meditation, he'd stroll down *Quai de la Megisserie* along the right bank of the Seine heading towards the Louvre. This walking tour he repeated every chance he'd had when in Paris. But this time he suddenly turned left onto *Pont Neuf,* crossed it and walked back eastward, now on the other side of the river, towards *Boulevard Saint Michelle* where he walked south until he reached the *Luxembourg Gardens*. It wasn't a short walk by any means, and it was very early in the morning, in March, and Paris was cold, wet and carbon monoxide laden.

In the gardens, under a gazebo completely covered by vegetation appearing to be crawling up and devouring its wooden columns, a school orchestra played with fierce passion and concentration a piece by Mozart…or was it Haydn? In any case he enjoyed this familiar yet unidentifiable piece of music, this unexpected bonus of cultural pleasure as he stood there. And standing there he saw Vladimir Guzman approaching, black suit, black suitcase and a fixed smile.

'The time has come for me to go back to Lima'. Vladimir Guzman said under a repressed shout and wider smile.

'I know'. Replied Aesma Daeva dry and indifferent; he was still trying to identify the name of the composer and composition; the more he heard it the closer he was, it seemed those names were hidden somewhere in the tip of his tongue.

'I think I should fly down there as soon as possible and make a statement to the media'. Aesma Daeva remained quiet without even acknowledging his concern. Vladimir stared at him confused and a little irritated.

'Is there something wrong?' Vladimir tried to see what he was staring at, and only saw a bunch of kids playing music, he turned to him and before he could pronounce a word the other turned to him.

'If you tell me who composed that piece we'll be in Lima tonight'. Aesma Daeva declared without taking his ice-blue eyes away from the young orchestra.

'Excuse me?' Vladimir had heard what he said but didn't understand what he meant.

'If you tell me who composed the piece they're performing, -he pointed with a slight movement of the head towards the group of kids- we'll be in Lima by tonight'. Vladimir turned once again to the school orchestra and turned back to him, he smiled.

'Are you serious? Why that would be Mozart's Eine Kleine Nacht Musik, everyone knows that'.

He paused and without blinking he turned to look him in the eyes for the first time.

'You are absolutely right Vladimir, everyone should know that'. Letting a sigh of relief escape his chest, like a burp that after being trapped with no hope in the esophagus is finally rocketed out and released into the ether, he changed his posture, his tone more relaxed now.

'How long has it been, Vladimir my friend, since you've been back in Lima?' This time he actually noticed his eyes. Vladimir's eyes were pitch black but in this drizzling morning seemed to have a dark translucence feature, like tinted windows into his eager soul.

'It's been a little over four years'. When he answered he felt the coldness of Aesma Daeva's penetrating ice-blue eyes. They slowly began walking away.

'We're right on schedule then'. Vladimir nodded with impatience and delight.

'Everything happened sooner than expected. We must act swiftly and decidedly'. Aesma Daeva placed his cold and large hand on his shoulder.

'Don't worry, time is on our side'. He said and paused, Vladimir, a known Rolling Stones junkie, had to comment on that.

'Should I tell you who played that piece as well?' His question carried the sarcasm that was typical of him. The other had to smile.

'No, I think I know who, for I had many dinners with him'. Both smiled a sinister smile, one denoting more mischief than the other.

'Did you know him back when he wrote Sympathy for the Devil?' Asked Vladimir with true curiosity. As far as he was concerned, the school orchestra had stopped playing, the bird had quit singing, the air had ceased to blow, and the sky had decided to suddenly give up its crying.

'If you really listen to it, you will know'.

At the first sight of the first sign that spelled Atlanta, Lara Walker finally relaxed; she finally let go: her shoulders hung, her head bowed and rocked, her eyes reposed, her breathing slowed and became soothing, but her grip on the leather suitcase never loosened. She remembered as she dreamed. She dreamed of being in Lima and remembered shooting someone, or was it the other way around? Anyhow, she remembered being there, and maybe, dreamed about feeling sick after too many Pisco Sours that late at night. It was around 3:00 am but the guys she was with hadn't had enough. Patty Echevarria was there as well, she remembered, or maybe she dreamed about her being there. She had had many dreams about Patty before.

Her heavy eyelids slightly opened, at least she thought they did, as the bus hit a bump on the road; it had gotten so dark so fast and the interior of the bus seemed so quiet now, only the murmur of the movie being played on the tiny TVs screwed on the roof, and the tamed roar of the engine could've kept her awake but instead, they combined into a soothing hum numbing her awareness and rocking her in and out of dreamland. She dreamed about a taxi cab, and the four of them squashed in the back seat; she remembered laughing out loud, Patty half way sitting on her lap, Gustavo offering his and Milenko pulling out some coke.

After he was done eating, Francis, his co-manager and long time friend, handed him a restaurant shirt, dry pants -both part of the uniform for the staff-, and sandals which curiously enough happened to be his. Once dressed she told him he had to come with her, to her place she said. He followed quietly. Only then did service go back to normal and the few tables that had shown up that weird Sunday -usually on Sundays it was a full house-, were taken cared of again. Just a while earlier all Servers and Busboys had abandoned the floor leaving Johanna, the Hostess, as the only staff member in front of the house; even the cooks evacuated the kitchen, putting on hold all the orders until they all took a look at Timothy Moone or Mr. Tim as they called him; their boss.

Timothy Moone's sudden reappearance had certainly shaken everyone who worked there, and especially Francis who had been running the restaurant all by herself, with no knowledge whatsoever of Timothy's whereabouts or whether he was still alive or dead. Everyone wanted to be in the manager's office, Timothy's office, where Francis cleaned, hugged and asked him so many questions that it only made him the more confused and hungrier. After he was done eating she was going to take him home. Did he remember where home was? Umm, he didn't know exactly, well neither did she. So it was her place then. Johanna, the Hostess, was to take care of the restaurant until she came back, after all, they only had three lousy tables on this lousy Sunday.

There was much gossip and speculation about his whereabouts and disappearance and shocking reappearance amongst the busboys, servers and dishwashers, whom exchanged exaggerated theories with the cooks; the whole restaurant was left buzzing with whispers and tales, and to no surprise, since Timothy Moone was the owner of the restaurant who managed it side by side with Francis, and the last thing everyone had heard about him was that he had gone on a business trip to Egypt, but never came back.

She also dreamed with the smell of *anticuchos.* She remembered heading to the bohemian district of *Barranco,* where once, the artists of the day, would hang around in the main strip, sided by old bars and pubs, reeking beer and cork, and they'd debate, deliberate, write and draw inspiration from the cigarette smoke and the pitcher of beer, and the irredeemable love; now is the epicenter of a malnourished and fragile rock movement and busy narcotics haven. And eventhough the district of Barranco have been systematically invaded by posers and garbage, gangs and dirt, it still, somehow, manages to radiate its artistic spirit and bohemian celebration.

The bus slowed down and all the nerves in her body became aware once again. She dazedly looked out the window and saw Atlanta.

He didn't remember her did he? She was Francis: manager of his restaurant for two years, the only manager, besides him, that ever worked there, his right hand, his friend, his…occasional lover. He didn't remember anything? What was it amnesia? What'd happened to him? She stared at his bruises, scars and wounds; especially the one in his forehead that seem fresh and glistening. Francis couldn't remain sitting on the couch, she lit a cigarette, took a couple of drags and tried to sit again. Timothy for his part, sat still in his quiet confusion, he couldn't understand why if she was who she said she was, why she seemed more upset rather than glad to see him.

How about if *she'd* tell him what had happened, maybe he'll remember something; for instance, since when was he missing? He was supposed to be back here about a month ago she told him. She knew he had to travel somewhere, Egypt maybe, but on the date he was supposed be back at work he hadn't shown up at the restaurant, didn't answered or returned any of her calls, or anyone else's for that matter. She'd actually thought that he had taken off somewhere else or maybe extended his trip, but as time went by and there was no sign, no call, no messages, she then knew there was something wrong. He didn't just do those kind of things, she said to him, she knew him enough to think that he was just gonna take off without informing her when was he planning to return or discussing the restaurant's itinerary in his absence; nothing! no, that wasn't his style. Did he *even* remember traveling? Timothy seemed to make an honest attempt at wanting to remember but he didn't. His mind was like thick fog over a dark swamp when suddenly he heard voices in his head. The voices came as boiling bubbles of mud rising to the surface with intensity, unintelligible and violent, strange and painful. He cringed and let out a moan taking his hands to his skull, trying to pinpoint with his fingertips the area of this odd pain, but it seemed to be coming from the middle of the inside of his head, somewhere right behind his eyes. It wasn't pain but it hurt. And just when he thought his head was going to burst, it was gone, and his mind was left in blank with one sole image floating from where the pain had come from; the image of the woman in the white robe.

As the bus slowly ended its uneventful odyssey and starting pulling up into its designated space, Lara Walker mentally travelled once again to Lima, to that particular night, to the four of them walking through the strip, the bohemian boulevard, that lead them to the main park, where clusters of people of different ages -mostly underage- would just stand there drinking and telling jokes, others to see and be seen, but mostly it served as the crossroads for buyers and sellers of some of the highest quality cocaine -at unbeatable prices- in the world. The scent of *anticuchos* being cooked on custom made flat tops on wooden carts, pushed by those ladies reputed to be the best in the city, engulfed them, lured them, hypnotized them…and there they stood watching how these ladies cut, skewed, sauted, turned, seasoned, turned again and served those juicy and beefy heart kebobs.

On the steps of *El Puente de los Suspiros,* a narrow and short wooden bridge, that brings one to the other side of Barranco, notorious for being a spot where friends become lovers and lovers sigh romance, they sat to eat. She remembered how she closed her eyes and tried to detect all those intricate, meaty and velvety flavors dancing in her mouth. That night she liked Lima. The City of Kings.

Francis returned to the restaurant two hours later, emotionally exhausted by the day's events but especially by the strange and violent headache that Timothy suffered back there. Luckily so far they'd only done twenty covers and were just about to close, despite all the fuss and commotion the staff had done their job well but they still had one hundred questions about Timothy. She knew as much as they did: just that Timothy had a severe case of amnesia apparently, but only a doctor could determine that, for now they'd have to wait and see what happens. Back at her condo, Timothy Moone stepped in the shower. The longest shower ever taken in recorded history; he washed himself, he scrapped himself, he got on his knees and started to cry: his moans were muffled by the fury of the shower, his tears dissolved in the hot water and became steam, his frustration and dirt dripped from his body clogging the tub.

Outside in the balcony, overlooking the gray ocean, he meditated again: he thought of white. The night had a nice cool breeze, rare in the month of June, and the therapeutic sounds of the waves only enhanced his meditation, which would've been complete if it wasn't for the sizzling in his forehead. Timothy sat in lotus position ignoring the pain. He regulated his breathing, his heartbeats; he reorganized his brain's data bank slowly, calmly but surely. And he saw white; he felt white. Whiteness all around him, enveloping him in a cool bubble. White was infinite…it was openness, it was cleanliness…He felt much better, he saw clearer. He actually saw scenes in his head thought deleted a little while ago: He saw the white tower, the white building, the white hotel, the white door, the white towels on the floor, the white sheets, the white panties, the white robe, the white lines on the glass surface, the white packets in the black suitcase. He suddenly opened his eyes: He saw black.

At the station Lara walked to a payphone and pressed the numbers written in a wrinkled scrap of paper she took from her back pocket. Eddie's number. As she dialed her eyes were discretely scanning the place for anyone slightly suspicious; her gun had its safety off and was easily accessible. She finished dialing. One, two rings she looked to her left; three, four, she looked to her right; five, six, she turned around; seven, eight, a voice came on the other side: hello?

Gino Gianoli

San Francisco, U.S.

Room 606 was quaint and cozy but desperately small for two unknown personalities. Patricia Echevarria arrived first at the Savoy Hotel and checked in at around 5:00 pm. Timothy Moone was to knock on the door almost two hours later.

Seven cigarettes, four beers and a lousy movie later, the knocks were heard. Patty's bile was at its boiling point and some foam could've been forming under her tongue. She waited for the second round of precise knockings. They were a bit louder this time.

'Yes?' She asked.

'Hi dear'. Was the reply agreed upon.

'It's about fucking time!' She said as she slammed the door.

'My apologies, but I wasn't timely notified.' He dropped the suitcase on the bed, queen size single bed, took a look around the room and the one bed, stuck his head into the bathroom and with an expression that denoted nothing but distress and disappointment; he dropped on the bed.

'Man, this is tiny. Who…who was in charge of this?'

Order Out of Chaos

'What should I call you?' She asked him as she popped open the suitcase, taking out a pile of files, documents and photographs.

'Faust, call me Faust'. He replied with no will as he walked into the bathroom and turned the shower on. Patty halted her studies of the files and leaned forward to see if this guy was actually taking a shower with the door opened. Who the hell does he think he is! Just as she was beginning to follow the trail of clothes thrown on the tile floor, a chopped intonation of David Bowie's 'Let's Dance' bounced off the bathrooms walls into her horrified ears.

The bathroom door was then heard slammed shut.

Later that night they went out to dinner to the Grand Cafe just a couple blocks down on *Geary Street*. Patty looked radiant with a splash of a long gone spanish aristocratic nonchalance, while Timothy resembled a young millionaire internet entrepreneur in its peak of glory, in the midst of conquests and infinite possibilities.

'Aren't you worry that that'd give you a full blown heart attack, Faust?' She pointed with her caramel eyes at the two pieces of sauted Foie Gras swimming in blueberry chutney.

'Timothy, my name is Timothy, Patricia'. He took another bite and let the velvety and buttery texture spread all over his mouth, he simply replied with a loud and clear: Mmmmmm.

'How did you know my…oh forget it'.

Some time later, this scent, this unmistakable aroma would lead him through a dark alley back into his restaurant, back into his previous life.

Back in the tiny hotel room, they got to work. The photographs were laid out on the bed, addresses and other assortments of codes were entered in a laptop computer and the two plane tickets to Lima were confirmed. Patty informed him about a third contact who was already waiting there, and when she revealed that this contact was also a girl, Timothy commented to himself:

'As long as she has an appetite we'll be fine'. Referring to Patty's meal that night: No appetizer, a plain mixed greens salad for entree and yogurt with berries for dessert, and water, with no ice. Well, the four beers she had drank while waiting for his arrival had replaced lunch and dinner as far as she was concerned.

He stared at the photograph of the new Target. He knew exactly who he was eventhough it was the first time he'd seen his face. So, this is how you look he murmured.

'What?' Patty asked as she walked out of the bathroom after a shower. 'What you say?'. He took another long look at the photo and then threw it on the bed where it landed on a pile of more photographs.

'Patricia, you're Peruvian aren't you?' She unrolled the towel off her hair and walked back into the bathroom.

'You certainly know a lot about me.' She slanted towards the mirror applying cream on her face. 'What else do you know, I bet you don't know how old I am? He heard her echoed voice and smiled at the sarcasm; he walked around the bed and into the bathroom and found her face all covered in white.

'I wouldn't dared to even guess your age out loud'.

'Good! You're a smart guy Faust'.

'Timothy'.

'Oh yeah, Timothy, sorry'. She kept rubbing more cream on her forehead. 'Wasn't Timothy a disciple of Jesus?'

'I don't know, I think he was a disciple of Paul.'

'Who's Paul?'

'Some guy in the Bible,' He held one of the photographs in his hand.

'Are you the religious type? She said rubbing her chin now.

'What, what makes you say that?'

'You seem to know about the Bible and the disciples and—'

'Just because I knew that Timothy was a disciple of Paul doesn't mean—'

'Alright, alright, don't get all upset now, I didn't mean to—'

'Listen, that's not important, what I wanna know is what do you think about this guy?' Without turning as she rinsed her face she said:

'I think he deserves what he's gonna get'.

'He's that bad ha?'

'No, he's worse.' She turn the faucet off and covered her face with a towel.

The pile of photographs, about fifty of them, all had Vladimir Garzon's face printed on.

Chiclayo, Peru

Months before Patricia Echevarria met Timothy Moone at the Savoy Hotel in San Francisco, she met with an anonymous man at the legendary Fiesta Restaurant for a typical northern-peruvian breakfast and to acquire a videocassette with a very interesting recording. The breakfast consisted of fresh papaya juice, a sweet version of tamales called here Humitas and freshly baked rolls. The videotape contained irrefutable and undeniable illegal dealings by none other than President Ignacio Valverde himself.

This anonymous man introduced himself as Rocoto Relleno: a chubby, dark-skinned man, with post-acne cheeks and a painted smile. He sat and, while devouring six Humitas, related the latest archaeological findings at the pre-Inca site of the Lord of Sipan. Apparently, some grave robbers, while digging in an old pyramid looking for any remains of artifacts unnoticed or unburied by the archaeologists, stumbled upon a untouched funeral chamber which they couldn't believed their eyes: A neatly preserved mummified corpse of another noble lord covered completely in gold and precious stones. Around him the remains of two sacrificed maidens, and what it looked like a dog, were clearly displayed and arranged, along with baskets of dried two-thousand-year-old grains.

He took a break from eating and talking at the same time. Then he continued eating.

...Fortunately the police and members of the archaeological team apprehended these robbers as they were looting the timeless grave, as they've done and keep doing so often. The funny thing is that the archaeologists were tipped off by the wife of one of the robbers when she found out that her husband had another family beside her and their kids; There was another wife and three kids, living in a house, supported by him and residing in the same town. Scorned and revengeful she called the Institute of Archaeology and related to them what she had overheard when the group of grave robbers gathered that same morning to plan the theft.

Patty listened, and nodded, she had payed attention and understood. She had heard about the new findings at that historical site, she'd been there a few months prior to this breakfast, taking a part of a university excursion for her archaeology classes. She was interested in the latest Sipan news alright, but she had to inquire about his name.

She knew that Rocoto Relleno was the name of a traditional dish from the city of Arequipa, which literally meant Stuffed Peppers, and she wanted to know why would someone call himself that. His replied was that she was absolutely right in her observation about the dish being traditional of Arequipa and all, but it wasn't a nickname or a code name. It was his christian and legal name.

'How can you be named after a dish?'

'My parents loved that dish, I think they were addicted to it, may they rest in peace, I don't blame them, it is very tasty'.

'Yes…but that's not a legal name…is it?'

'Maybe in Lima, señorita, but where I come from there is not such thing as an illegal name'.

Whether he was pulling her leg or not, we'd never know for sure, in any case, he did resembled an overcooked stuffed pepper, but they weren't here there to discuss the legality of certain names, or the relationship of the name to the resemblance of the person bearing it; they were there for more serious reasons.

She could've swear that the chubby man flirted with her throughout their meeting, but then again, the men of Chiclayo were reputed to be charming sexual predators until the day they'd die; many of them had two and three separate families; not mistresses but whole families on the side, it was accepted by society as long as one didn't get caught.

This inoffensively short and stocky, harmlessly funny-looking man was to hand her a sinister envelope containing a poisonous videotape with a shocking recording of a secret meeting in the Presidential Palace. The recording clearly shows President Ignacio Valverde, his advisors and seven Senators from several opposition parties, sitting in one of the more private rooms of the Palace, never before seen on a recording, in a circle cracking jokes, smoking cigars, sipping on cognac and whatnot. Until that point, the only strange thing about the recording would have been the President sitting in the same room with those senators, known detractors of his administration. Minutes later we can see one of the Presidential Advisors talking, in a serious tone now, the reason why they're there. Then a zoom takes us much closer to witness how those Senators are being bribed to change stands and votes, in favor of the ruling party, of course. These votes were needed to have a majority in Congress thus making it easier for the President to seek reelection, thanks to all the new laws that would be 'swiftly approved' by Congress. These new laws obviously would be very popular in their nature: increment in salaries, construction of new schools and roads, etc. even if the country couldn't have afforded those measures, the people would be happy, and the Presidential Elections were just a year away, and that was all that mattered. The stacks of bills are seen being handed and distributed amongst the participants of this clandestine partnership. After the lewd transactions are made, it is sealed with symbolic handshakes and hollow hugs. Some obligatory last minute jokes were said and then with ear-to-ear smiles they were all sent off. At the end of the recording, one can clearly see President Valverde and his advisors making a toast, in obvious satisfaction, as a pre-celebration of his reelection, and a final comment by the President that would become as infamous as the video itself. Raising his glass of scotch he added with shameless nonchalance: 'Another hard day at work, salud'.

But before Patty would leave the restaurant and see the contents of this tape, Rocoto Relleno came back to the topic of the Lord of Sipan findings.

'You know señorita, that the more I think about those sites, the pyramids I mean, the more I wonder'.

'What do you mean exactly?' Said Patty.

'You know, pyramids here, in Mexico, in Egypt, some say that there are even pyramids in China, How come?'

'Maybe,' Patty thought as she spoke. 'these people had some universal knowledge, who knows'.

Both seemed to have forgotten their original business and intrigued by these interesting facts.

'You know, señorita, that the Incas represented Viracocha, their supreme man-god, as tall, pale and blue-eyed and thought he had come by the sea, taught them about civilization and society and gave them knowledge, then he parted promising to return one day. That's why, when the Spaniards came it was so easy to conquer the Inca Empire for they thought they were related to Viracocha, they thought they were gods'. Rocoto Relleno drew a wide chubby smile and finished drinking his coffee, he knew that the señorita sitting in front of him was definitely hooked on his conversation.

'What do you know, exactly, about the civilization that built those pyramids?' Patty inquired putting the envelope inside her bag.

'All I know,' Began Rocoto Relleno asking for another cup of coffee. 'is that the people who lived in the Lambayeque valley, where the pyramids are situated have a legend of a lord whom they called Naylamp. He, like Viracocha, arrived in a balsa or a raft made of straw, and he settled here and built palaces. His followers worshiped him as a god and when he died he was buried in a pyramid, and legend goes that he flew away. He was succeeded by eleven generations of kings whom all were buried in pyramids. This recent discovery, the one I was telling you about, is just the second one, imagine. But this all came to an end with Fempellec, the last of the kings whose tragic end was followed by a severe drought. Then, another tribe, the Moche, resided in these plains but were conquered by the

Chimu, the ones who built the Chan Chan Fortress, an amazing piece of ancient architecture, have you ever seen it señorita?

'I'm afraid I haven't'. Replied Patty a bit embarrassed.

'Oh, but you must. One must dig into his ancient roots to see himself at the beginning and at the end of time. But where was I?...Oh the Chimu. Well, the Chimu had its own legends and gods, very similar to the previous civilizations' gods and myths: they all came from the sea, with some great knowledge and the leader was always tall pale with blue eyes. And so the Chimu people where conquered by the Incas whose civilization was so vast that it needed two capitals cities: Cuzco and Quito. The rest of the story I am sure you know it señorita. This cycles and transitions and transfers of knowledge came to an end with the coming of the Spanish and their Bible'.

Looking at her watch, Patty excused herself, got up and left. Rocoto Relleno was left semi-standing, like the semi-gentlemen he was, with that chubby smile of his. He ordered another coffee.

Before she took a taxi to the airport, Patty thought about going to the pre-Inca site, where that hollow, eroded pyramid stood and its once noble corpses were disturbed from their peaceful sleep and dug out and displayed in front of school children, or smuggled to some European country where there it, too, would be displayed in front of much older children, but she didn't have enough time for a cultural detour, but perhaps just enough for a culinary one. She headed to the *Plaza de Armas* where she'd heard of a little restaurant -that consisted of the transformed living and dining rooms of an old colonial house- where the best black conch ceviche was made right in front of one's face, really spicy and potentially deadly.

Miami Beach, U.S.

As Patty swallowed that last piquant and aphrodisiac mollusk, and slurped the black liquid essence that was to revive her soul and clear her sinus, Timothy Moone and Francis Green were getting the staff ready for service. In less than an hour the restaurant would be open for service and still some tables weren't properly set. The reservation book was filled with names and numbers in such a messy fashion that not even the people who deciphered the Rosetta Stone would've been able to read this. There were reservations for several large parties which caused the rearrangements of tables, since some of them had to be put together in order to accommodate the groups. The staff ran out of silverware and table clothes to reset later while the bartender bitched for more glasses. But none of that mattered, it had been a while since they were overbooked and it was going to be a hell of a night, financially. Then, when nothing else could go wrong, Francis told him that one of the servers had called in sick and they had no one to replace him with. She told him that a replacement was definitely needed and fast, or else they'd be buried by the first hour of service. He was panicking now, irritated but concentrated; he thought of jumping on the floor himself as a server, but Francis wouldn't have been able to manage the whole restaurant by herself. What was he to do? He was in deep shit.

With a couple of bumps of blow he tried to clear his head, and he did. He had six busboys and four servers, he needed one more. He asked the bartender, the hostess, the dishwasher, everyone, if they knew anyone who'd wanna make serious money tonight. He estimated around three to four hundred per server on a night like this. Johanna, the hostess, was freaking out as well since it was impossible for her to make a realistic floor plan when they were missing a server and the tables were constantly changing. Johanna, we don't wanna hear it, you do what you gotta do and that's it.

One of the busboys, Serge was his name, suggested to Timothy, or Mr.Tim as they'd call him, the appointment of one of the busboys to be a server for that night, since they were six, moving one of them up would leave five busboys and five servers. Of course Serge was expecting himself to be chosen, to be temporarily promoted, plus, he knew the basics and had a good personality. Mr.Tim had to think about it. But really, he didn't have to.

Later that night, much, much later, Timothy jumped in his pool and floated looking at the starless sky and sighing a sigh of relief. All his muscles relaxed as the tension drained from them like blood from a bullet wound. Weightless, numb, unburdened, he enjoyed his silence; released, appeased, he looked within; loosed and alone, he imagined being a baby; a fetus; an embryo in a womb; protected, sheltered and covered from the dirt and pain of this reality. He felt all this as he floated, he felt it more than the average joe for he was an artist, and the point of being an artist was to feel beyond, beneath and above the ordinary threshold of sensation.

Timothy Moone was a writer that was never published, a painter that painted half way through, a poet that never found a final prose…Only in the restaurant business did he find some sort of fulfillment, a sort of needed accomplishment; that ever slippery satisfaction of finishing something, that elusive vision of the culmination of a project, of a plan, of a dream…and eventhough it wasn't his life's passion, he had to, and he was, making the best of it, for he knew that only the Lucky ones loved what they did; the Happy ones had learned to love what they do.

Gazing at the moonless sky, he actually felt as if he was floating in space. Meditation made him the more relaxed now; it had been a hectic night. Two hundred and fifty covers were welcomed, sat, fed and sent on their way, breaking the year old record of two hundred. Even with Serge as a server, he had to jump in and help take orders, bring cocktails, take plates out of the kitchen, pour water, open bottles of wine, bring checks and clear and reset tables, in order to keep the boat afloat. And it remained afloat. It was a good night for he felt self- satisfaction. Then he thought of Francis.

He didn't know what he felt for her. What was it? Lust, sexual friendship, indebtedness for all she've done for him, admiration for her devotion to him and his restaurant, or pity at the sight of such a beautiful woman so alone, so desperately looking for someone to give him all the love she had in her immense heart. Francis was a great woman in his eyes, she was physically luring, with her wavy blonde hair, perfect milky skin, and naughty looks; her well rounded breasts stood proud and, at times, insolent; her inappropriate sexual whispers while working became addictive; the casual rubbing of her skin against his became more frequent, and the carnal hours in the office, after everyone had gone, became longer and louder.

But his real concern was not what he felt for her but what *she* felt fot him. Afterall, she was first his coworker and comanager, someone very important for his business; he didn't want, eventhough it wasn't up to him anymore, that this…thing, this fling they had, to get in the way of business. In the back of his mind there was a voice that told him it was too late, he had broken a cardinal rule: don't shit where you eat.

And then the phone rang. It was five in the morning.

Gino Gianoli

Timothy paced up and down the condo mumbling words to himself: asking and replying, swearing and cursing. He wanted to remember. He needed to remember. A black suitcase and the woman in a white robe were the only barely discernible images in his convulsive mind. Shapes and colors appeared, blury landscapes, fleeting glimpses of things that were once clear memories, fogged his mind's eye. It all arrived at a slow pace to then recede back into the abyss to remain blank again. He forced himself to think white again, he tried to meditate but couldn't relax; frustration made his blood boil, his neurons pop like pop corn, and the round scar in his forehead palpitate. Then, little by little a hemorrhage of images, sounds, smells and emotions came rushing back, like a tidal wave, to the front of his mind becoming almost unbearable, almost painful to the point where he had to scream and consequently collapse in the middle of the living room, but before he passed out completely he managed to crawl to the sofa.

In his dream state, he heard the voices again: they howled at him words and noises in such high pitch that it made his ears bleed. They weren't boiling mud bubbles in a dark swamp anymore, they were a thousand microscopic killer bees buzzing and stinging at his eardrums.

He looked so different, Lara thought. Eddie was tall and chubby, super-white with red hair, a few freckles scattered on his round and serious, almost hairless face; he looked so young, he was young; but he looked younger. He stood in front of her in his oversized hip-hop attire probably thinking the same thing: She looks so different; and from behind his eyes lust started creeping in, and he couldn't believe the woman standing in front of him, in tight black leather pants and long sleeve shirt was the same Lara he used to kiss and touch. What was she doing here? And why was her outfit more New York than Miami. But no time to talk, she was in trouble and needed a place to crash for a few days, and…she had a proposition…business…if he was interested of course. If he could make money out of it, he was interested. He wanted to help her with her only bag and the suitcase but she refused rudely; then she apologized and said it was okay, she could manage her bag and the suitcase; took one last look around and lead the way out. Atlanta smelled different somehow she thought.

Later that night Francis Green returned to her condo, on the eleventh floor of the Ocean View Towers on Collins Ave. to find Timothy passed out on her couch. She approached him slowly, remembering, with every step she took, passages, scenes of them together: at dinner, in her condo watching a movie, making love -to her they had sex only the first time, the following encounters they'd made love-, cooking, walking on the beach…

She sat on the sofa next to him and contemplated his beaten body; his arms bruised, his legs scratched and cut, his chest, bony, with his ribs more pronounced, and that weird wound in his forehead, that kept getting redder and redder; she tried to place her finger on it, but it was still open, it hadn't scabbed yet.

She wasn't his official girlfriend, just a good friend, a close friend she thought, emotionally close. They had one of those don't-ask-don't-tell kind of relationships, where both drivers refuse to take ahold of the steering wheel to lead the car to any particular direction, instead they let go of the wheel and enjoy the ride regardless of the destination. But Francis Green was a woman of many recourses, let's just say that she'd secretly activated the Cruise Control so the ride wouldn't careen off the road and would last longer than it should've.

She realized that eventhough she had shared with him some of her life, some secrets, many dreams and plans; she still didn't know much about him; basic information a girlfriend should have, like where he lived; but she wasn't his girlfriend. She started working for him a couple of years back but only in the past six months did their relationship shifted from the professional to the erotic; she knew that sometimes he travelled for business; she also knew he lived on the beach but never been invited - something she still resented-; she knew he was in his late twenties early thirties but didn't know exactly how old or if he had any family or even friends. The only thing she was sure was that he wasn't married or engaged or had an official girlfriend. He couldn't have. But why was she thinking all this now? Did she just realized that the possibility of love was always there. She was still in denial: Love stopped being a possibility and became a reality the moment she looked forward to go to work and dreaded her days off; or, had she been lying to herself thinking that he could love her as much as she did, when he'd never given her a spoken declaration, or even insinuation, of reciprocal love, other than recurrent sex. But to Francis Green actions spoke louder than words and judging by their long conversations, the way he looked at her, the tenderness in his caress and other small important details, the possibility of mutual love had been there; but now her world had been turned upside down.

When they got on the expressway Lara broke the thin ice by asking about his mother, saint aunt Marlene. She died, answered him dry and emotionless, his head still bouncing to the loud beat of the music. He'd heard hers had died too. He liked her mom he said, she was always more easy going than his. She knew what he meant; all that religion and stuff, drove her crazy, fanatic, and him ultimately into becoming an atheist. To tell her the truth he couldn't take it anylonger, he'd left the house before he turned eighteen. Lara remained silent, Eddie kept bouncing his head. When did her mother died? He wanted to know. A while back she said, as dry and emotionless as her cousin.

He drove his '01 Mustang proud. She liked it ha? Baby had nitro and everything, baby hauled ass. Yeah it was nice and all, but she wasn't there to talk cars and nitro. The reason why she was there was because she needed to get out of Miami, and the

Order Out of Chaos

reason she called him was to see if he could help her get rid of the stuff that was in the suitcase. After a brief moment of silence and him blinking back and forth from the road to her, he nodded as if he was thinking of something. What is it that's in there?

Eddie, had he ever heard of something called the Breakfast of Gods? His cheeks stopped being chubby and became long, his freckles turned as white as his face. Breakfast of...he whispered to himself. Yeah, had he heard of that? the new cocaine? She raised her voice. Of course he'd heard about that what did she think he was...this may not be Miami but...Alright, alright, so? Did he think he could help her sell it? How much she got in there? A lot, she couldn't help smile, a whole bunch of it, as he would say. And she stoled the whole bunch right? Yes, that's right. And now they were looking all over for her? Mhm, yes. And if they'd find her they'd kill her right? Mhm, yes, but they won't, if we get rid of it fast, Eddie. Oh lord, they were in trouble Eddie understated, dry and emotionless.

He opened his eyes but he wasn't awake. The shape of the voices were still visible in his retina. For a nanosecond he didn't know where he was and thought that the nightmare had started all over again, and then he saw her, lying next to him, sleeping. And seeing her like this he felt somehow he'd seen that delicate face before, just like that: sleeping. Her name and who she was he had to learn again but her face seemed strangely familiar now: Her mouth slightly opened, her blonde wavy hair spread on her pillow on both sides, like butterfly wings; she looked so peaceful, so devoted, so…beautiful. Yes, she had brought him here last night. The restaurant. Yes, he knew how she tasted, she was his girlfriend maybe, or his wife? No, he didn't remember having a wife, then again, he didn't remember much of anything. Images were coming and going. He thought of grabbing a pen and paper and write them down as they'd arrived. But he didn't move, he just stared up the ceiling fan and suddenly remember being in Lima.

By now he had clues if not about his life, about his activities: a trip to Egypt -why would he go to Egypt though?; the woman in the white robe and the black suitcase, most likely drugs, the restaurant and her, Francis, the woman lying next to him. The memory that didn't come alone and with the most pieces to put together was Lima -so apparently he's been to Peru and Egypt so far. He got there during the night…He'd had some problems with his baggage…At the airport he took a taxi to the Hotel El Condado…Entered his suite…The phone rang. That's it.

Alexandria, Egypt

What would the great classical architect Dinocrates say, if he'd walk through Alexandria today? Would he complain about the weather or the carbon monoxide? Would he complain about the noise from the hundreds and thousands of people walking its retail crowded streets, or from those bulldozers and cranes demolishing the old and elegant while erecting new and strange edifices? And what would he say if he had to wait outside, by the front steps of the new Library -which nostalgically attempts to bring back the honor and prestige and, why not, some of the myth of its ill-fated ancestor, the classic Library whose exact location is still a mystery to us- for a contact that was forty minutes late, having just arrived after flying for eleven hours, tired, thirsty, on a 90 degrees fahrenheit afternoon, with a bag containing twenty kilos of cocaine? He would have asked mighty Alexander to behead this unprofessional contact and burn the city he helped build.

So, before Timothy answered the phone, before he was floating in his pool at five in the morning, before he installed that pool, before he even bought that house, and before, way before -two and a half years to be precise- he acquired that restaurant, he was here; standing at the front steps of the new Library in Alexandria, carrying twenty kilos of cocaine, waiting for a frenchman, a contact called Bernard.

After two cigarettes and an insincere apology, they stopped in *El Bashwat* street at a cozy typical cafe at Bernard's request. And eventhough Paradise Cafe offered a decent array of pastries and baked goods, it was the real food the frenchman was after, Timothy just wanted a tall glass of Coke and a quick refill.

'So, have you seen to the Mosque yet?' The french asked with a slight British accent in a very casual way as if they knew each other forever.

'No, I haven't, is it nice?' He answered uninterested and bothered. Was it the heat? The people? He wanted a refill.

'It's beautiful yes, very nice, but you can't come in if you're not Muslim, are you?' Timothy felt just like a stranger in a strange land, and eventhough one could consider him well-travelled, there was something about this city that he didn't trust; the looks; the loud voices; the language? He peeped into his cup and the ice had become water and pretty soon it would become air. Bernard, having attended when he was younger a Hospitality School in Switzerland for a few years in hope of becoming an Hotelier like his father, noticed the lack of service and demanded something in French to the fat man behind the counter, hopefully Timothy's refill.

Two men in suits walked by their table, mumbled something in, was it French? Arab? it was too fast and too low to determine which, and stepped inside the Cafe, then stopped to talk to the fat man behind the counter, who kept looking at their little table outside. Bernard seem unalarmed. The two men went through a little door behind the big fat man. There were other people sitting in the other tables, they didn't look Egyptian or Arab for that matter; maybe they were tourists.

'Is there something wrong?' Timothy asked tightening his grip to the bag.

'Ahh, don't worry, they're one of us'. Bernard lit a cigarette and discretely nodded to the fat man behind the counter making his eyes sparkle and head nod in reply, while Timothy's hand slowly headed for his gun. The air was suffocatingly thick and the moment increasingly intense.

'What are we doing here anyways?' He appeared upset. 'Can we go somewhere indoors, it's fucking hot out here'.

Bernard put the just-lit cigarette out, got up and motioned Timothy to come with him. He softened the grip of his gun.

'No, no leave the bag here, it's ok, it's ok'. Timothy was getting up but hesitated, stopped, halted, froze; his heart wasn't running, it was hauling ass.

'What do you mean leave it here? I'm not leaving anything here'. His grip tightened once again. The fat man from behind the counter stepped out and started approaching their table, the people on the next table, the tourists, stopped their eating and chatting to stare at them. Bernard was standing, lighting another cigarette with all the time in the world and looking around, blinking his eyes and furrowing his brows on and off, apparently disappointed, while Timothy was halfway sitting halfway standing, with one hand holding the bag on his lap and against his chest, and the other gripping his gun hidden in between. The big fat man approached the table and said something to Bernard who kept puffing not looking at him, it sounded like bitching, as if the fat man was scare or worried or something. Then turned to Timothy who had finally decided to sit back and remain as cool as he could ever be.

'My friend, no problem, me? you? me with you? your people, me your people'. Bernard smiled.

'I told you, they're with us, leave the bag here, relax.' He said it very slowly, being careful of pronouncing each word as if Timothy didn't understand English. The fat man's face was of a pleading kind, he kept looking inside the Cafe and back at Timothy and the bag. Bernard gave a last drag out of the cigarette and motioned Timothy to stop being an asshole and just hand over the bag.

'C'mon cowboy, let me show you around town'. The air felt loose and light, almost purifying. He smiled and lifted his hands as in ok, no problem.

'Money in hotel'. Said the big fat man, taking the bag and walking back behind the counter with an uttermost effort.

As they walked through the streets crowded with people, shops and Coca-Cola billboards, Bernard lit another cigarette.

'What was that in there? I thought you knew how to work with these Arabs?' Timothy kept silent, he was happy it was over, but he was also exhausted and irritated.

'First, I had long and horrible flight, then, finally I get here and have to wait, under the unbearable heat, an hour for you!'

'Thirty minutes!' Interjected Bernard.

'Forty minutes!' Corrected Timothy. 'To then be immediately taken to do the transaction with people I hadn't even met! So I guess I didn't know how to deal these Arabs!' Bernard kept quiet but wanted to laugh badly.

'And where are we going anyways?!' Timothy seemed about to breakdown crying and Bernard couldn't hold it anymore. He burst out laughing and Timothy had no choice but to laugh too.

Later, in a more decent restaurant inside the hotel, Timothy told him it was his first time on that side of the world. Bernard looked surprised.
'First time? I thought you americans were everywhere in the world'.
'Well, we're not, and it's also my first and last time working with you guys'. He drank his coffee. Bernard lit yet another cigarette.
'Ooh you're hurting my feelings'. He ordered another Cognac.
'How many cigarettes do you smoke a day?'
'Oh please don't start with that shit, you americans are all the same, as soon as you stop liking something, you expect the rest of the world to stop liking it too, fuck you'. Timothy drew a tired smiled and asked for the check.
'I gotta tell you though,' He started saying to Bernard. 'you'll never know how close that fat man got to getting shot, even you too!' Bernard bursted out his signature raspy laugh that quickly turned into multiple coughs. He was choking and he liked it.
'Us? no, no, no my american cowboy, *you* will never know how close *your throat* got from being ripped out, ha, ha, don't you fuck with these Arabs'. They both had to laugh.

'Really?, and who was gonna slit my throat?' He asked him for a cigarette.

'I thought you didn't smoke?'

'I never said I didn't; it was you, in your typical french arrogance, who *assumed* I didn't smoke'. Bernard had to smile, nodded his head and handed one, then lit it.

'So tell me, who was gonna slit my throat?'

'I'll tell you who: Remember the people on the other table? they had two guns pointing at you when I got up and signaled them it was ok, then when Karim, the fat man, was trying to get the bag from you, there were two other young men behind you that just were waiting for Karim's signal to ssslit your CocaCola throat'. His face turned serious and bland.

'But everything came out ok, don't you think marlboro man?' Timothy didn't answer; again the air had become thick and unbreathable. 'Now, when you arrive in your room, look in the closet, in the compartment to the left there will be an envelope with enough money to make your boss happy'. Timothy was surprised, and he couldn't deny it.

'Well...' Timothy got up.

'Well, tomorrow I shall show you around this beautiful city, go on and sleep tight marlboro man, after tomorrow you will never forget Alexandria'.

They shook hands and Bernard gave him another cigarette, for later, he said.

    The next day he awoke tired. He had slept the rest of previous day, the whole night, the whole morning and now it was four o'clock in the afternoon and the alarm was going off. But it wasn't the alarm really, it was the telephone, and it was Bernard calling. Half an hour later they met down in the lobby, and headed off to visit the Mosque of *Mursuit Abou-Al-Abas* that was just as beautiful and intriguing as Lara's eyes. Eyes he was yet to meet. There, they talked about the nature of their business, religion, women, and politics. Bernard had to be *the* funniest guy Timothy had ever met; he had a smart answer to everything and seemed sincere and straight forward. If he didn't like something he would let you know even if you didn't ask or didn't care. Then he asked him if he'd ever heard of Aesma Daeva.
    As far as Timothy was concerned he had only heard that name once, when, along with a British colleague of his, they smuggled a substantial amount of heroin from South America to Spain. There, in an old tavern in the town of Alicante, his British pal, Colin, related to him what he had heard about Aesma Daeva: that he lived somewhere in Germany and headed the largest organization ever known. This organization, according to Colin,

spread from the States to China; quote, unquote. Bernard for his part, had also heard similar stories and conspiracy theories where the name Aesma Daeva seemed to come up frequently, but he was skeptical by nature and thought of it, if true at all, to be just an alias that someone invented to protect its own name that just took a life of its own. But even Bernard couldn't deny that the people that he worked for, were very far from the top of the pyramid.

'Don't you think so?' Timothy by then had just been invited to worked for a small organization, focused mostly on the drug trade. But this small organization was part of a conglomerate of small organizations united to protect each other's interests. That was as far as Timothy, and everyone else there knew. What they couldn't have known, because only an selected few did, was that this conglomerate was ran by a larger organization of officials from different regions of the world. These officials usually held a high rank position in their country's government or ran its biggest and most important companies; and that's as far as those selected few ever knew. They didn't know that the only way for those people to get to those positions and become officials, is by being personally appointed or recommended by a member of the Lower Council, with the unanimous approval of the Higher Council, the Council of Thirteen, which was headed by Aesma Daeva.

As it was usual, none had ever seem him but had heard their share of stories and rumors concerning his dubious existence and ubiquitous prominence. To talk about Aesma Daeva was to talk about an entity, as ethereal as God and as influential as the Devil.

They walked another long conversation on their way to the Roman Amphitheater at *Kom-Al-Dikkah*. Such conversation revolved around future side projects that didn't have to involve unnecessary participants. Timothy heard the French as he demonstrated with an accurate and elastic use of the English language, at why they'd had to do it and how they'd go about doing it. There were many, many people here, hungry to get ahold of more of this new cocaine, demand is just too large!

'Hold up, hold up, what do you mean by *new* cocaine?' Timothy asked confused and Bernard turned serious for the first time. 'What's *new* about it?'

Bernard paused for a few seconds.

'It is more powerful than the regular one, that is all'. They kept walking and he went on to explain how if they only could get rid of the middle people, they'd be able to offer more and at less prices, thus assuring them a few good returning clients, and best of all: he'd got the contact; some big shot politician in South America. As good as it sounded, the danger was too great; and while Timothy thought about it, Bernard was left baffled by the american's question about what was new in this cocaine; maybe he was fucking with him, to test him or something. These americans are all the same, he thought.

Back at the lobby Bernard asked him what he thought about what they talked about tonight. Timothy politely declined and thanked him anyway.

'Too risky'. He said to him.

'To be alive is risky'. Answered Bernard lighting a cigarette.

'To tell you the truth, this city is pretty and all but, I really don't think I'll be back here'.

The phone call at five in the morning will prove him wrong.

Lima, Peru

When Anais Echevarria called for a press conference at her office in Congress, she had underestimated the power of the Media. The unofficial fourth power of the State, the Media, in these electronically driven times, is sometimes more powerful than the official three, for it possesses the power to manipulate people's opinions and perceptions, and everyone knows and accepts, and the ones who can, use that power to accomplish their goal. So when Senator Echevarria was asked, before the press conference had even began, about the infamous video, she was caught offguard, cold and stiff. In all of her years in public office she had never been so surprised, so astonished, so shocked at the realization of the real extension of its power. She hadn't told a soul about the damn video, it was exclusive news for the reporters, how the hell did they know? But she didn't fret for too long, for she realized that this was something that didn't belong to her, this was beyond exclusivity and personal spotlighting; this was a national catastrophe, a political earthquake; this was more than a Presidential embarrassment and impeachment; this meant prosecution and jail.

Order Out of Chaos

The media might have somehow gotten a tip -and that in itself, no doubt had dark origins- and known about the existence of a inculpatory videotape of some high ranking government official, but they didn't know exactly who. Moreover, the people on the streets didn't know, had no idea what they were about to hear. Even worse, the President himself would be fishing in the Amazon as Senator Echevarria pressed the play button to show the reporters and the country and the world, how this man turned public money into conscience money and how the 'Fathers of the Nation' -as Senators and Congress men were called- became the 'Thieves of the Nation' -a headline that would be printed on various newspapers the morning after.

The can of worms had been pried open. Her three phone lines couldn't handle the endless influx on calls. Her cellular phone ran out of battery from the constant ringing, her office door cracked at the incessant knockings and its bronze handle quickly turned black from the continuous turning.

She was now officially inside the ring and the bell had rung.

While many women in her country dreamed of finding prince charming -with the right last name and enough cash- and be married by no later than twenty-five, to stay home with the kids and wait for their husband, who'd most likely work in a office or a bank, to come back home everynight, Anais dreamed of becoming the first woman President of her country. Perhaps her foreign education and experiences broadened her perception of life and reality, and as such, this broad mentality would clash with the narrow Latin perception of the role of women in society. But as imminent as it is, time changes everything and everyone. No matter how stubborn or strong, how deep and rooted, how traditional or universal, change it's just a matter of time.

She tried to call her daughter, Patty, at her cellular phone but no luck. She wanted to share this ambivalent news with her; her only family. These were great news for it meant the end of a corrupted administration, but at the same time they were sad as well; what did this tragedy say about them as a society? She thought. About their way of life, their perception of life. She guessed that people would see this as nothing new. That they went from a bad one to a worse one. The only real difference was that it was the first time that they could actually watch the crime on the television. Jose Carlos, her late husband, knew this would happen. He knew that Valverde, if elected, would be the continuation of Guzman but with a different face; this country needed new people up there, clean people with no ties to any organization or the traditional political parties. He had the answer and he had the will. And his chance came when Vladimir Guzman fled the country and immediate elections were summoned.

He was going to get elected, he knew it, Anais knew it, the country knew it, Ignacio Valverde knew it and Aesma Daeva knew it. But all his possibilities abruptly vanished that windy and drizzling morning on his way back from the supermarket. Thus clearing the way for Valverde to be elected President and four years later the main protagonist of the by now, world-viewed video. His five year term would end a year too soon by tomorrow.

An interesting fact is that four years prior, her husband, Presidential candidate Echevarria's car got intersected by two white vans and himself taken out and thrown onto the wet street, he thought he'd heard the voice of a girl, not of a woman, of a girl; behind that long, black and cold gun barrel pointing at his forehead. He could've swear it was something in Italian what he heard before he saw a blinding flash.

By the time she arrived home late that night, a swarm of reporters and cameras and lights and microphones rushed and surrounded her big black car, a relentless mob starving for extra information, comments, interjections, expressions, anything that can later be analyzed and dissected by the 'political commentators' on TV. With the help of her newly appointed body guards, she managed to get into her house and breathe. Patty was standing there with a complex facial expression denoting surprise, gladness, confusion, worry and understanding.

'The President just resigned on television'. Patty said as she hugged her thin and overwhelmed mother. 'And you were the reason why, mom'.

Anais paused for a second and turned to the television set where news anchors, talkshow hosts, political analysts and anyone who had anything to say on TV, were having a field day.

'No Patty, *greed* is the reason why he had to resign. Greed.'

After running the video images time after time after time, in slow motion, pausing when the infamous Senators are receiving the stacks of bills, zooming on the faces, freezing it when they're toasting, and repeating the President's infamous last phrase, they, the analysts, began informing about recent investigations on the falsehood of the many charges against ex-President Vladimir Guzman and a possible conspiracy, by the deposed Valverde administration, to take not only the presidency from him but his life as well...and, as if that wasn't enough, a recent document that may link Valverde's people to the murder, four years ago, of candidate Jose Carlos Echevarria, was being analyzed by the experts. All this and much more would come after the brief messages.

Anais Echevarria felt coldness invading her head first and then her whole body. Patty sat unaffected by the commentary on TV, by the supposition that her father could've been murdered by people linked to Valverde. It came as to no shock to her. Her father *was* murdered, that was no news for her, but, was it him? she didn't think so. Her mother excused herself and headed for the bathroom.

Looking into the toilet bowl, on her knees she prepared for the storm ahead and with that thought, a hot bath would be just and necessary.

A list of questions that she'd put on hold came now screaming and rattled in her mind: Who filmed this? Even more intriguing: Why and who sent it to her? and How did they know this was taking place at that particular time, and that particular place? And how did they filmed this? These questions lingered in her mind as she sank in the warm thick soap. She closed her eyes.

Gino Gianoli

Paris, France

Anais slowly leaned back, closed her eyes and let the hot bubbly water massage her tense muscles; at that same instant across the Atlantic and seven hours ahead, Vladimir Guzman and Aesma Daeva walked out of the *Jardin du Luxembourg* as the school orchestra played Faure's 'Pastorale' from 'Masques et Bergamasques' as an indirect and implicit congratulatory coda.

But before Aesma Daeva would make any last minute flight arrangements, the two enigmatic men walked all the way to the Cemetery of Montparnasse, there still was plenty of time.

They walked through the picturesque boulevard as the businesses started to open and the scent of brewing coffee and freshly baked pastries came and went; Aesma Daeva's cellular phone wouldn't stop ringing and receiving urgent e-mail messages explaining the latest developments on the Valverde corruption scandal and last-minute polls on Guzman's return approval. A slight drizzle began to envelope the two three-piece-suit-wearing gentlemen as they strolled on through the grey and chilly morning. Past the main gates and the directory of famous people buried there, the two men slowly marched on the narrow and flat dirt paths that crisscrossed the cemetery.

Vladimir thought about his father, and how he didn't know where he was buried, moreover, how he'd never made any attempts at finding out; it was better that way; afterall, he didn't even get to know him. He thought about death. He thought about his mother and the blury memories of her. He thought about a child, traveling in an old smelly bus to Lima from hours away, a piece of paper in his pocket, as important as his life, contained the address where he would grow into an adult. The face of the tall grandfather, as seen from a child's perspective, followed immediately. Then he thought about his life: the events that molded it, the dreams that fueled it, and the destiny that guided it. Staring at those tombs made him feel the more alive, the more real. He breathed and he was aware of it, he could see and he was aware of it; at that moment, nothing was taken for granted.

'Take a look Vladimir, this is the grave of Cesar Vallejo'. He pointed with his chin to the large marble tomb. 'One of the greatest, if not *the* greatest, peruvian poet'.

Vladimir approached the tombstone inside what resembled a miniature chapel. He stared at the stone long and hard, as if he was trying to see beyond that granite lid, as if he possessed some kind of x-ray vision; but at the impossibility of this, he just let his imagination described how Mr.Vallejo might've looked like that foggy and humid Parisian morning. Then they wandered through the other graves: some were grand, detailed and ornamented; their epitaphs eloquent, standing tall and proud, perhaps as a representation of the person that now rested underneath; others were simple, minimalistic, austere, they gave a sense of loneliness and sadness; but they all spoke of the eternal reality of the End.

Some people mourned in silence, alone, staring and speaking to the engraved stones in front of them, their eyes red, swollen, their heads down, their flowers positioned underneath the carved name of the deceased, the thin drizzle unnoticed, the hours passing them by.

'When you die, where would you like to be buried?' Asked Aesma Daeva walking next to Vladimir.

'I've never really given that thought…a thought'. He answered mindlessly.

'Well, give it a thought now'. More than a mere philosophical suggestion, to Vladimir it resounded in his mind as a velvety demand. 'What better environment to think about one's own end than this one'. He finished saying and his phone rang again. While he spoke a few steps away in some kind of dialect or strange language, it would be fair to say that Vladimir was left a bit disturbed, to say the least, at the connotation of this conversation. But all that was rapidly dissolved when Aesma Daeva flipped his phone and told him the limousine was outside the cemetery waiting for them. Inside, warm and comforting, they sat facing each other.

'The things one must do for his country; it must be hard being a President'. His ice-blue eyes didn't blink, but the sound of his voice carried some irony. The car silently drove back through the boulevard.

'It must be hard being you'. Vladimir answered with the same irony. Aesma Daeva looked at his watch, looked out the window, and back at him.

'You get used to it'. They both smile without a sound.

Later that night he boarded a private plane that would take him to New York, from where he would embark to Lima, where he would be welcomed back by the people and the press as some kind of victim-hero that has finally returned to save the day.

Gino Gianoli

The morning brought a splitting headache and a sore and itchy body, but Timothy Moone felt happy, he had regained some clear memories, though too few to be put in context, but more were expected to come in due time. He walked out of the bedroom and had traded the restaurant's low quality tuxedo pants for a pair of checkered pajamas that were too short for him, but much more comfortable. Francis called him to the kitchen table for breakfast and couldn't help smiling at the sight of this skinny man, with ruffled blue hair, in her pajamas that fitted him like Capri pants, approaching her like a confused little kid.

Midway through breakfast Francis' soft and once again worried words floated into his ear. 'Do you remember ever being in Fisher Island? Timothy

Moone stopped eating, he remembered thinking about it at the pier.

'You went there once, about a year, a year and a half ago, to visit someone; he sounded important, like he worked for the Government or something'. Timothy sat upright and looked the other way, while she gazed at him; worried, inquiring.

'Do you remember anything about this?'

The morning was bright and clear but his head still damped and foggy. But he did remember something. Sort of.

How many times had he been there? he thought. When Francis took him and had to stay in the car while he boarded the ferry and was taken to the Mansion; that was the second time he'd been there. The first time, god knows how long ago, he gave his name to the guard and took the ferry. Inside the Mansion he waited in the studio facing a wide wooden desk, the room smelled like vintage cigar. It all felt expensive, aristocratic, powerful. He recognized the two Matisses on either side of the wall and a Chagall right behind where he stood, hanging straight across the enormous desk made out of cedar with strange ornaments, tiny eyes and pyramids, on its shiny surface. Right behind it the imposing chair, that looked more like a throne than a chair, and the endless rows of books and tomes, files and documents; they all blended imperceptibly with the exquisite decor of the spacious studio. But Timothy Moone didn't remember this. Nor did he remember he was just about to open his own restaurant on Ocean Drive, with money from his other not so worthy activities; and it was for this reason, for his exceptional abilities in the smuggling and murder-for-hire fields that he was invited to meet with someone that would introduce him to a large, powerful and invisible world.

The day following her arrival they went out to the city to get rid of the stuff. Eddie's contacts were eager to see but unable to buy that kind of merchandise. Hours later, after much driving and tedious waiting they left downtown Atlanta mortified and famished. Three places visited, three turndowns; some of them just wanted to see something they'd never seen, others didn't even want to see the merchandise or even talk about it and would rudely ask them to leave. Lara noticed hints of fear in their voices. A bit paranoid maybe Lara?

That evening Eddie invited her out for dinner and clubbing.

'I'll accept the former but need to think about the latter'. She said as she walked to the bathroom to take a shower; Eddie sat in the kitchen table rolling a joint.

'What the hell did you just say?' Lara was in no mood to party, it was Monday for crying out loud; and for all she knew there could be someone waiting on the roof for the right moment to take her out. Deep down, she always thought she'd end up like that. Karma?, not quite yet. After the shower they got ready to go. Lara didn't know whether to leave or take the suitcase with her. She vacillated for a while, then decided to stash it somewhere in the house. Outside Eddie waited in the car. The horn honked. 'I'm coming!'

The restaurant was in the same neighborhood where Eddie lived. It served Greek cuisine.

'What's the name of this place again?' She asked discretely looking around.

'Hendekakis'. He answered behind the menu cart while she thought that Greek should definitely be her next language to conquer; then she ordered the Gavras Salata and Octopodis tis Skaras for her entree, while Eddie ordered a boring Greek Salad and Galeos me Skordala. Lara asked him how come he knew so much about Greek food.

'I had a Greek girlfriend, she got me into this shit, by the way those grilled octopus tentacles are the bomb'. Lara took several bites of that chewy mollusk before finding it interesting first, and delicious later.

'Have you ever been there?'

'Where?' Eddie answered with his mouth full.
'Greece.'
'You kidding, I haven't even gotten out of Georgia'. Answer him while she thought of the blue sea against the white houses covering the hills; and she wished she'd be there.

As they ate, Eddie told her that he knew of a place she'd definitely like; it was a club, and on Mondays they played all that obscure Gothic rock.

'What makes you think I like Gothic rock?' She asked flattered, unconsciously associating the Gothic look with her younger years. He told her the black outfit gimmick gave her away.

'Last night you wore those same black leather pants, tonight is the *complete* leather outfit'. He said as he chewed his on his Shark on garlic sauce. She told him that she ran faster with those pants and boots.

'I didn't know we were gonna run tonight?' He said.

'You never know when you're going to run until you're running'. She replied lifting her glass of wine. 'And by the way, I do like Gothic rock'.

Afterwards they headed to the Midtown-Buckhead area.

How long had it been since she heard *The Sisters of Mercy* that loud? Hordes of lost souls dressed in black with black make-up and black nail polish jumping and turning, chanting and contorting their bodies with the music. The club was called Rarity Atlanta and it consisted of three dancefloors playing three different types of music, but tonight it was Gothic on all three levels. Lara with her black hair and black eyes and black leather outfit fitted just right. Eddie came from the bar holding two drinks with a cigarette barely held between his thin lips.

'You really like this vampire shit don't you?' He yelled and she nodded as her body followed the rhythms. She sipped her drink long and deep with her eyes closed and suddenly felt calmness washing her within; then she was back in Lima at the steps of *el Puente de los Suspiros*, savoring the meaty heart kebobs with Patty, Milenko and Gustavo.

An impeccable man in a dark-blue, four-button Armani suit spoke from behind him. 'Please to meet you at last Mr. Moone'.

He bided him to take a seat and offered a cigar from the intricately etched wooden humidor.

'No thank you.' Timothy paused and semi-sat uncomfortably. 'With all due respect,' He began right away. 'Why am I here and who are you?'

The slim and older figure sitting across him did take a cigar; he snipped its tip and began burning it with all the patience and pleasure in the world, then stared back at him, a deep stare that imposed respect and attention.

'You've been invited to join our club, or as we like to call it, our family; and you can call me Baphomet, to answer your first two questions'. The dry voice came from behind the thick fresh smoke and Timothy moved uncomfortably in the wide leather chair while the smoke slowly dissolved and the tanned face and slicked hair of the elder figure across him reappeared. 'And to answer your following two questions, first, our club is an organization of vast resources with many different interests in many different places; and second; the reason you've been invited is simply because we consider you to have certain abilities that we can put to use in our interests'. Timothy remained still and in silence. He stood up and walked around the desk leaving a thick trail of smoke lingering in mid air.

'We have observed how efficient, first; reliable, second; and trustworthy you are Mr. Moone; may I call you Timothy?' He nodded. 'And these are the attributes we look for in *all* the members of our organization. My dear Timothy, come please'.

The two of them walked out of the studio and into a courtyard of a terrace overlooking the infinite blueness of the ocean.

'I know that you have a thousand questions now, but they'll be all answered in due time, for now enjoy the view'. That would mark the first of many visits to the Mansion at Fisher Island.

She will never forget how from where they sat, in *el malecon*, they could've overlooked the Pacific Ocean only if it weren't so damn dark or so poorly lit. It was around 5:30 am and the roars and moans of the waves -these ones certainly qualified as waves- were becoming louder and clearer; they were hungry so it seemed; they were also imposing and threatening.

The last pitcher of beer evaporated and it was time to head back to Gustavo's house. Lara had become fond of him, he was a nice guy, simple and sincere; as opposed to Milenko, always trying to take advantage of every situation and everyone, and one never knew what he was thinking. But Lara, as observant as her profession required her to be, knew exactly what he was thinking. Patty also could tell that Milenko wanted to get into Lara's pants. Was it just women intuition or professional instinct?

Patty Echevarria was her main contact in Lima. And also the only one in the room that knew the real reason about Lara's visit to Peru. She was the one in charge of providing the latest movements of the Target in detail. Since they had worked together before they had become acquainted and took a real like to each other. So knowing that Lara was in town, Patty called two friends and the four went out to party.

Gustavo's house was located in the residential district of San Isidro right across from the golf course which he'd never seen or been at. There, he served what remained in an old bottle of rum. They all looked as if their batteries were running out, with nothing else to say, and slouching on the couch. Patty went to the kitchen to make a call to another contact that was supposed to have arrived to his hotel around that time. What time was it anyways? But Milenko refused to let the night end and pulled out the tiny packet of magazine paper folded in such manner that it resembled a miniature pillow. It seemed as no one else wanted to join him in a line of coke or deny the bird-chirping outside, the purplelish aura slipping through the blinds or the ever increasing frequency of cars passing by and the intensity of their roar. 'The imminent coming of a new dawn' said him. Followed by: 'Oh c'mon guys just a line each'. No one replied and Patty kept dialing the hotel. Then the sun bursted outside and as synchronized as they could be, both Gustavo and Milenko jumped to shut all the curtains close. In the kitchen Patty whispered to Lara that the call went through and the third contact had just arrived: An american she had just met in San Francisco two days prior, his name was Timothy Moone.

'Lara, hey Lara!' She opened her eyes and almost lost balance, the music seemed louder now, and being there at the club seemed as a bad dream. Slowly she became quasi-conscious and sort of recognized the song, a song by *Joy Division*. 'Good news,' said Eddie obviously intoxicated. 'Tomorrow we may have a buyer, some big shot from…I forget where they said he was from but that doesn't matter, I resolved your problem little cousin…' Lara took an urgent look around and all she could see were shadows, silhouettes rapidly moving and jumping, appearing and vanishing. She reached for the inside of her jacket to check her gun. After all, the people around them did look like vampires.

Silence woke him up. He turned and Francis wasn't there. What time was it? By the time he got out of bed he realized it was dark and he was naked. He walked to the kitchen and grabbed something to eat. The microwave clock marked 11:30 pm. He must've had gone back to sleep after breakfast, he thought. Francis is probably working. Walked back to the bedroom to find something to wear, he found her white pajama pants he wore that morning, and that's when the voices came back like an eagle of vengeance burying its sharp and long talons into his skull. He fell on his knees and his screams were muted, only the voices could be heard and they were louder than ever, they were screaming at him, they called out his name, he dropped to the floor covering his ears and banging his head against the floor, but the screeching voices came from within, he waited bent on his knees. Once they appeared to be gone, he went into her walking closet to find a shirt or whatever he can put on. He hurried out the bedroom into the living room towards the door but it was lock. He tried to turn the knob again; no! Yes Timothy it's locked from the outside. He uselessly punched and kicked the door, he was in no shape to bring it down, especially since it opened inwards. He paced up and down the condo, left to right, confused, disoriented; he tried again: locked Timothy, it's locked! Walked back and stepped out into the terrace. His blue hairs were stirred by the strong breeze; he looked down the veranda: eleven stories down to the kidney shape pool. He screamed.

Think, think…think goddamnit! He walked into and right out of the kitchen and into the bedroom. He didn't know what to look for, what to see, what to do…Timothy was locked in. He picked up the phone but who was he going to call? He knew no one; he remembered no one. Everything was going to be okay, he just needed to relax and think things through; there had to be an explanation for this, he thought, why would Francis lock the door? He sat on the floor not before trying to open it again one last time. He sat and waited; the wound in his forehead palpitated. And he waited some more, until a his mind became obscured by the thick fog of weakness. Then everything became heavy; blur caressed his vision while sleep whispered in his ear. The whisper made him dream two dreams.

In the first one he was walking down a dirt road in the middle of the desert; he seemed to have been walking for miles. Obviously tired and weakness fell upon him. As he found himself on his knees four men approached him, picked him up and took him to a cave. There he awoke recuperated and healthy, full of energy, to a warm fire. Right behind the dancing flames he could device the four faces of the men in hooded tunics. They all spoke to him, at once, like an amplified single voice: "You are the continuation. Make them follow". And right after he received that revelation he vomited all over himself.

In his second dream he went back to the Hotel El Condado in Lima. He had met with a pretty peruvian girl weeks before in San Francisco, what was her name? umm…Patricia! yes, Patricia. Yes, it was her who he was supposed to meet with and she was going to introduced him to the third contact. Oh yes…there she was…those black deep eyes, that black hair so shiny…that body so slim, those lips, those legs, that voice…

They had met on the afternoon following his arrival, in a churrasqueria in the district of *Barranco* for lunch; Patty set up the meeting and they were introduced. And eventhough Lara and Patty had stayed out all night with Milenko and Gustavo, and later went to bed together, it was the shower that took everything out of them; nevertheless they looked sharp and focus. Timothy Moone had checked in at 6:00 am and five minutes later he received a call from Patty, as previously planned. Now they were having lunch. Unofficial, friendly and casual lunch.

He took a cab back to his hotel and turned the news on. Funny how the news are slightly different in other countries he thought, it was very refreshing to watch and hear world news not from an American point of view. And as the news anchor blubbered about some presidential meeting to create an Asian Union just like the European one, and the plans to follow with another union of north, central and south America, Timothy only thought about Lara, and only heard Lara's words, what she had said at the table, and Lara's surreptitious looks and hidden smiles at him. Oh, he wanted to see her again. And he would, the following day.

And these memory-dreams kept replaying in his head one after the other, again and again in an endless circle as he sat on the floor, body jerking like a fish out of the water, eyes rolled back and foam forming in his mouth. That's how Francis found him when she walked in.

The next morning the phone was ringing. Eddie stuck his hand out from underneath the comforter and pressed End. It quit ringing. Right before his hand was back under the cover it started ringing once again. The latest incarnation of Beethoven's 'Für Elise' coming from the phone was loud and high toned -and to think of the many years of intensive study and solitude, of lessons and discipline to make his talent become genius, Ludwig Van had to go through, to end up as one of the many different ring tones of the day, right next to 'La Cucaracha'-. The once unique and beautiful melody resounded insulting and robotic, but to him, just annoying. He grabbed it and tried to take a look at the number of the incoming call, but his vision was blurry; so he answered.

Twenty minutes later they were both running out the door and into the car with, Lara carrying the suitcase and a backpack.

They headed northwest towards the Georgia Dome. Up Magnum street they stopped at a warehouse where, according to the one who called, the one Eddie met the night before at the club, the buyer and him would be waiting. Apparently this someone knew someone that knew someone.

They were tired and hung over, even the roar of the Mustang was weak and exhausted. After the dust cleared they looked at each other anxiously.

'Last stop Lara, what are we doing if I get turned down again?' She remained in silence, took another long look at the warehouse and asked him how well did he know those people.

'I told you there's someone in there that I know, he's waiting for me, he knows the buyer'. Lara shook her head in uneasiness.

'How long do you think this is going to take Eddie?' She couldn't let go of the suitcase.

'How the hell should I know? all I know, is that the longer we stay here the longer its gonna take'. Lara wasn't feeling good, her head was pounding and her mouth was dry. She couldn't think straight, she just wanted to get this thing over with, take a couple aspirins and go back to bed.

'Twenty minutes you hear? If in twenty minutes you're not out here in the car, I'm coming in'. Eddie smirked and stepped out of the car; immediately pulled his cellular phone and dialed. Two seconds after he flipped the phone a door opened; he bent into the driver's window.

'Alrighty superwoman, in twenty minutes you get in and shoot everybody'. Smirked again took the suitcase and walked inside.

There's nothing worse than disappointment she thought.

Her leg jerked repeatedly and continuously with impatience and anxiety, her head kept turning towards the door that had closed behind him. She was thirsty and nauseous; all she wanted was to go back to bed.

Memories of the night before mixed with the uncertainties of the moment at hand.

How long has it been? Eight minutes and counting. Out of the backpack she pulled out her .9mm, installed its silencer, checked the clip, cocked it and took a deep breath.

Gino Gianoli

Miami Beach, U.S.

Vladimir Guzman's private flight landed in JFK for refueling, just before five in the morning according to control tower's data. Before the wheels made contact with the pavement of the runway, he fished out his tiny cellular phone, and dialed a number that began with a 305 area code, a Miami number, Timothy Moone's number.

Timothy had mixed feelings about this plan. The pay would be more than generous, approximately three times as much as the regular ones, but - and there's always a but-, there were certain things that bothered him greatly. For one, he would have to travel back to Alexandria; god how long has it been two, three years? and of course the contact was the French Chimney, Bernard. He remembered him alright. The second thing was that he needed to be in the restaurant. Business had increased dramatically and more and more his presence was needed there, like last night. Francis and the staff did a great job, but without his help maybe it would've been a different story. And third, and this one bothered him the most, was that this operation would be conducted outside the official channels; it was going to be a 'side project' as Bernard called it, and the only ones involved would be the three of them. Vladimir was the connection to get the stuff out of Peru, Timothy would be the one to smuggle it all the way to Egypt, where Bernard would receive it and negotiate the sale with his contacts. No middlemen, less hands, more money. It sounded too good therefore too dangerous. He thought about it as he paced around the pool. It wasn't dark outside anymore, the sky had a purplelish hue rapidly turning orange. The voice on the other end had given him thirty minutes decide, they couldn't wait any longer than that, was he in or out? He had to refreshen his thoughts, he had ten minutes left before the phone rang again.

He made headway into the pool again. Underwater he realized the awkward position he found himself in; 'as a side project', 'only the three of us' Those words, those phrases, those commands, those dangerous and inviting propositions, kept playing again and again in his head. He didn't really need the money; but who doesn't need half a million! It was a lot of money they were talking about. But why were people paying so much for such a small quantity? Vladimir mentioned eleven to start.

Timothy Moone, a man with experience in the world of smuggling, didn't have a clue about the package he was asked to deliver.

Half a mil, his mind said and thought of the things he'd do. One trip, one delivery, that's it. But what about Francis, what would he say to her? He swam to the other end and rested in the corner, he didn't feel sleepy at all though he'd worked hard all night. The red plastic phone standing on the edge of the pool stared at him threatening to ring any minute now. He looked up the sky and saw the sun awaking, took a deep breath and submerged. No he couldn't do it. He couldn't leave the restaurant now. It was too dangerous. It was suicide. It was half a million dollars. One trip. Francis could handle it for a couple of days, couldn't she? Maybe they won't get busy until next weekend anyway. He'd be back by then for sure. Side project. Betrayal? No, just a side gig, nothing more. Just one delivery. Maybe this time he would go see those pyramids. He emerged from the silent, blury and slow underwater reality to a noisy, bright and uncertain morning: the air warm, the birds chirping away, the psshooing of garbage trucks, and his phone ringing.

Lima, Peru

Vladimir Guzman had hid in the trunk of a friend's car in order to escape to the airport. The police had raided his house arresting two men, members of his deposed government, shredding and burning documents. All the newspapers had convicted President Vladimir Guzman of corruption before the courts had even been properly notified of his indictment. The President had sent his wife and only daughter to Paris a week before, forecasting this scenario. Now, he didn't have time to prove his innocence, he had already been condemned by the Media and therefore, the people. They got to the airport, entered a private ramp and boarded a private jet to Buenos Aires where Aesma Daeva happened to be waiting. Documents involving him in bribery of officials and drugs and arms trafficking had surfaced a month before, making the situation unbearable and the government unstable. In less than a month, everything, Vladimir Guzman's empire of three years, came tumbling down. But he had escaped.

Protests in the streets quickly turned into riots and strikes flourished like a rash all over the country. In fact, the whole country became paralyzed. Officials of the Guzman Administration were resigning left and right leaving the public offices vacant. It took two weeks for Congress to appoint an interim Government to handle the country's pending affairs and to convoke General Elections as soon as possible. A month later the candidates were officially announced and properly registered. There were nine official candidates running for President, but only two had clear chances: Jose Carlos Echevarria and Ignacio Valverde. Both offered a change in mentality and management and a break with the traditional politicians and their parties. While they were campaigning and promising, inflation was getting frightening high and recession didn't give any signals of movement. Not to mention criminality was on its record high, and the middle class on the brink of extinction. In this circumstances Lara Walker found Lima. Lima the Ugly.

She sat on a bench in the *Plaza Mayor* photographing a student riot in front of the Presidential Palace. The students were hopelessly demanding hope. While that was taking place, in front of City Hall, municipal workers were shouting justice be done, they hadn't been paid in six months. In the background, almost comically, the Archbishop was holding an open air prayer to end the chaos and revolts, amid the black smoke from the burning of tires blocking the main streets. Through another street, a different mob of protesters joined the students in their chants demanding the end of corruption, the apprehension and incarceration of the fugitive President, and of course, the raise of salaries. The day was grey but the forecast was certainly black.

It was a complete and absolute chaos that dirty afternoon. Along with the manifestations, Lara Walker photographed the main entrances of the Presidential Palace and City Hall; all the streets that lead to the Plaza and the military and police presence in the area. Then, through the telephoto lens she sighted and old beat up, blue Toyota Corolla. Inside there were two men. One in the driver's seat, the other in the back. They were looking straight at her. As she put her camera away in her backpack, she approached the car. It wasn't a car, it was a rusted chassis, with blue spots, and four wheels.

'Does this thing actually drive?' She asked the men inside in perfect peruvian spanish.

'Señorita Walker, you'd be surprise'. Said a chubby dark-skinned man with post-acne cheeks and a painted smile. He introduced himself as Rocoto Relleno.

Gino Gianoli

Four years before he met Patty Echevarria in a restaurant in Chiclayo to take part in the destruction of Ignacio Valverde's political career; Rocoto Relleno met Lara Walker in Lima, to be a key element in the ending of Jose Carlos Echevarria's Life.

The driver swirled, stopped half an inch from the car in front, changed lanes back and forth, ran two red lights, cursed a police man, an old woman and a street dog, double parked to piss behind a tree, a bush would be the correct definition according to Lara, then, hopped back on the car and continued his reckless automovilistic maneuvering until they finally arrived to a two story house in the district of *Chorrillos*, that by the way it appeared, it seemed as if the owner changed his mind midway and had left it like that, or ran out of money and couldn't finish building it completely; the house was halfway done and a lot of the building materials were laid around the front and back. There, in that makeshift house, the last preparations would take place.

The following morning Lima awoke angrier and dirtier. Riots were becoming greater and spread to other parts of the city. That morning, banks and many foodstores didn't open. Small retail shops were emptied by its owners for fear of looting, the larger ones had private guards that resembled military personnel, with automatic machine guns and bulletproof trucks. Uncertainty was smelled in the air. The night before, Presidential Candidate Ignacio Valverde arrived in a public manifestation demanding clean elections and promising radical changes if elected President. While Candidate Echevarria had appeared on a political TV show displaying his plan of government. They both agreed on bringing ex-President-now-fugitive Vladimir Guzman from wherever he was to face the charges attributed to him and his people.

Lara Walker and five others stepped out from the back of the house into two white vans. The twenty minute drive got them to an address in the district of *La Molina*. They drove by the front of the house where a lonely police car stood.

The address: Got it. Blue print of the house: Got it. Number of family members: three. Number of service personnel:three. Number of police officers or other protection personnel: two.

'That's it?' Lara asked dumfounded. 'Damn!'. All this and other important information was provided by none other than our friend Rocoto Relleno. The vans parked three houses away. They had the telephone company logo painted on the sides: *Telefonica del Peru* .

Fourteen minutes earlier Anais Echevarria was told by the maid that the chauffeur was feeling sick in his quarters, apparently he had fever, and they needed milk and fresh bread for breakfast. If she'd only knew how to drive she'd go to the market and the bakery herself but she didn't. Anais was ready to take the keys and go herself but her husband, Jose Carlos, insisted on him going to get milk and bread.

'I haven't done that in a while'. He said taking the keys from her.

'Are the officers taking you honey?'. Anais asked a little concerned.

'Honey, please, how ridiculous would that look; I'm going to show up to the store with bodyguards to buy milk. It's just gonna take me twenty minutes max, I promise. Here give me a kiss'.

Inside the vans preparations were taking place to proceed with the main plan: Home invasion. First they'd take the two police officers; piece of cake; twenty seconds; then, open the garage door with remote; twenty nine seconds. You take the back, you take the left side, you—Suddenly the garage door is heard, and then, seen opening slowly; they all look at each other. Immediately they communicate with the other van via radio. No, they don't know anything about it either. Lara Walker tightened the silencer and cocked her gun. Everyone else soon followed. There was a whisper: *La gringa esta loca*. Shhh! They all froze, stared in silence. No breathing was heard. Lara Walker's deep black eyes dilated, her grip tightened and one single gulp of saliva was heard, only by her, being swallowed down her throat.

A car pulled out. The black Accura, described in one of the documents Rocoto Relleno handed to them, was seen by everyone, and if they weren't mistaking, the Target himself was driving it. They waited. The voice on the radio asked for new orders, the reply was to wait. The garage door closed and the black Accura stopped next to the patrol car, exchanged conversations with the officers and took off. The voice on the radio confirmed that the Target was indeed driving. The black Accura rode down the street and made a quick right. The first van followed. The second took the parallel street.

'Still waiting for notification of new plan'. Said the voice from the second van. In the first van, where Lara Walker was, they agreed on the alternative plan: Intersection. Immediately they communicated the change to the others. They trailed the Target into the parking lot of a supermarket. There they waited. They saw him go into the store and, after fifteen minutes, come out. They resumed the trailing.

While the radio talk-show host debated with a political analyst about the present political situation, Jose Carlos Echevarria sensed, he actually felt, that his time had come to take the Presidency. He allowed himself to smile a satisfied smile, to thank God for this chance; a chance to change his country; to *save* his country. He was a conscious man though, he knew he hadn't won anything yet, he couldn't think of himself as victorious yet…not just yet. But he had to smile. He thought about the first things he'd do as President; he'd actually had come up with a list of things that should be taken care of immediately: the restructure of the social system, the fortification and reaffirmation of this feeble democracy, the firm resolution for the eradication of the coca leaf…Suddenly a loud screech: his right foot pressed on the breaks; a white van blocking the front and another one the back.

He hadn't realized what was happening because everything happened too fast. Only when he felt the coldness and harshness of the concrete street and saw into the barrel of a long, black gun, he knew his time had come, of course, not in the way he would've liked to. He thought of Patty and Anais. Their identical smiles.

In the out-of-focus background of the long, cold and ominous .9mm, his eyes caught the contours of a small oval shape covered by a mask, a ski-mask.

With great effort he saw the eyes: Large and round, black and abysmal, wicked and warm. Then, he heard something; they were words; a sentence; a phrase maybe? In his mind it took a while for him to realize what the person pointing the gun at his head had pronounced, but in reality it took less than a nanosecond. The whole scenario, a good eight seconds perhaps. But to him it was in slow motion. The words he heard, although not in his native spanish, were clearly understood and its undeniable meaning accepted with resignation: *Il suo tempo e venuto*;…and then the silent blinding flash.

The muffled noise was loud enough to startled and evict a whole colony of birds out of the surrounding trees and caused the neighborhood dogs to howl and moan. Strangely enough, the gray and dirty clouds released themselves in an unprecedented downpour.

The soulless body of a promising being, with the potential, and most important, the will, to change the status quo, laid there on the cold, and now wet, concrete; its eyes still screamed out a silent help, the blood was constantly washed from his forehead by the falling rain, making the bullet hole resembled a third eye, his hands opened and its fingers contracted, his lips wet by the rain but dried of life, his body just laid there…alone…while inside the black Accura the milk was turning sour.

So as the milk turned sour, and the morbidly curious had gathered around the body which by now was covered by newspapers and photographed by early-bird reporters catching the exclusive, Timothy Moone was boarding the ferry that was to take him to Fisher Island, to the Mansion, where he would meet Baphomet; and Vladimir Guzman had just been granted Political Asylum by the French Government, a month after the speech given by Aesma Daeva to the Council of Thirteen.

Order Out of Chaos

The sun was weak; the breeze got tired; the silence and waiting became terribly uncomfortable and Lara stepped out of the car with her .9mm as an extension of her arm. She slowly approached the entrance where, fifteen minutes earlier, Eddie had gone in through, but the door was locked. Hurried around the back where three old model Cadillacs were parked. There were two metal doors: rusted and corroded, one worse than the other. She ran back to the car and took a small knife from the same backpack she took the gun out of. It took her less than ten seconds to open it.

Inside she heard voices and its echoes; she took one step at a time in darkness. Eddie you fucking amateur she thought. Her body became a machine, a device to detect movement, voices, scents, with the sole purpose getting of the suitcase back; long gone was the hangover. Her eyes scanned the dark warehouse aided by a few streaks of light from the roof. There were different levels and the voices were heard all around. She kept silently advancing, moving in and out of the darkness. Suddenly a silhouette, a shadow amongst shadows was detected…Her breathing stopped, her eyes widened, her muscles contracted and her gun shot. A muffled beep and the shadow dropped. A thin trail of smoke coming out of the silencer hole was the only evidence that she had just shot someone. She approached the body: A chubby man, mid-forties, mustache. She kept walking.

On the second level the voices were traced to a room, or an office all the way in the back. There was a whole array of voices and she distinguished and counted five as she climbed the corroded iron stairs. Two men were standing outside the office talking to each other, oblivious to the conversations and the going ons that were taking place and what hid in the dark. She looked for more men but it was just them. She pointed her gun at each, back and forth, forth and back as she whispered one…two…one…two…and as her finger applied pressure to the trigger she heard Eddie's voice followed by the dark vision of him being dragged out of the office by two men and handed to the two that were about to be shot by her. She had to blink and regroup her focus.

When Francis walked through the door and found Timothy Moone in a heavy state of convulsion, she immediately dialed 911 and held his head up, in her arms as to avoid him choking on his vomit. She started calling onto him, yelling his name, between tears and cries. Timothy seemed to be in and out of consciousness even as he coughed and as they waited for emergency rescue, she heard him trying to tell her something. She wiped his face and mouth and told him to speak. 'Speak to me!' His eyes kept rolling back but he murmured something. Her name. She asked him what was it, what did he wanna say? He kept repeating her name.
'Yes, I'm listening Timothy, I'm here'.
'Lately,' Said Timothy as he stopped coughing. 'I've been…hearing voices in my head'.
'What kind of voices, what do they say?' She asked wiping the tears off her cheek.
'I, I don't understand what they say…but…I know what they want'. He started coughing and spitting again, and his face felt hot, fever was rising. Francis of course thought he was delirious, talking about hearing voices and that they want him and nonsense, but she encouraged him to talk more.

'What do they want Timothy, what do they want?'

'You know...I started to remember, but now it's not important anymore...to remember...'. Cold sweat invaded his body and his temperature kept getting higher. 'Francis...I remember who you are, I remember your love for me...'.

Francis couldn't hold back the overflow of tears that welled in her eyes and drained, like an open faucet, so much out of her that she felt light headed and dizzy. And just as she couldn't stop crying Timothy couldn't stop talking, it looked as if he was about to die right there and then and needed to say what he felt, or as if he was high on something and words were just being spat and coughed out in a delusionary catharsis.

'I will make them follow...the men in the cave told me to...make them follow'. She just stared at him with pity and happiness. Suddenly the paramedics rushed in taking Timothy from her and strapping him in the stretcher. Timothy, lost in the midst of his convulsions kept talking incoherently about time running out, and the truth, the real truth. Just before being wheeled into the ambulance, he lifted his head and saw Francis standing there.

'I won't forget you twice'. He said to her and the last thing she managed to see, before the backdoors were shut, was his almost perfectly round scar in his forehead.

And it seemed as if a whole day had passed since she hid behind the stairs and saw the group of men come down dragging her cousin along. When one of them turned a spotlight on, a long rectangular table appeared and she noticed that they were all wearing suits. She started counting how many stood there around the table, one…two…three…then she saw one of them pulling out a gun and pointing it to Eddie's head. She immediately pointed her gun to him and was about to pull the trigger when she heard her name.
It was alright she could come out, the voice said, and the group of men covered in half shadows, all turned to where she hid. But that couldn't be! she thought, they can't see me. And indeed they couldn't, but they didn't need to, they *knew* she was there. It was alright, the voice said again, but she would have to stop pointing and drop her gun, please. Her heart didn't know whether to stop or to beat even faster, her brain was aware of what was happening but couldn't comprehend, was she imagining this? how could…She heard her name again. This time a slim man stepped out of the shadows and into the light; from where she stood, behind the stairs, she could see that he was slim,

well dressed, his hair slicked back and his posture imposing.

'Now come out Ms. Walker, and hand over your gun'. He took a few steps in her direction and stopped when he felt, since he couldn't see, her gun pointing to his head. But she had to close her eyes to reality; she knew what this was about, here's where the running around stops. Her brain whispered the end, and with her eyes still closed she remembered when she was a child, in her mother's arms: warm, clean, protected…The blury image of her daddy, young and strong, handsome and kind, came and cross-dissolved into Timothy's smile and blue hair and crazy ideas…

'Lara come out!' Eddie pleaded with desperation and reproach. And with a final sigh she stepped out of the shelter of darkness, into their unpredictable light; hands in the air, gun tossed in front of her, and resigned to accept that her own weakness had caught up with her. *They only hunt when they know who to hunt'*. She knew better. Her hands were handcuffed swiftly and immediately, then, on her knees she thought what day was it? What time is it?

The slim figure approached her slowly and she remained silent, only her breathing was heard. He looked down at her, placed his hand on his face covering his mouth and began rubbing his cheeks as if he was debating with himself what to do next.

'Obviously Ms. Walker, you know what this situation means; obviously you know who we are, your silence only proves that'. He said with a clean accent. Everyone was silent, silence all around, only Eddie's moans now and then could be heard, but even that seemed far away. He lit a cigar and puffed away, walked around her a couple of times. Behind the thick smell of tobacco she could distinguish his real scent: dense, refined, masculine, paternal…He got down to her eye-level and blew smoke on her face.

'Ms. Walker, my name is Baphomet, please to meet you at last dear, we've been looking all over for you'.

Gino Gianoli

Baden-Baden, Germany

The black Mercedez glided silently through the Black Forest; Aesma Daeva cushioned in the back stared at his familiar and strange surroundings. He'd always had a certain longing for this ancient thermal village. Had he forgotten his childhood memories here? It hadn't changed that much; it never changed or if it did, it changed slowly…too slowly. The Black Forest he thought. He always used to imagined being lost in there. It terrified and excited him. His ice-blue eyes were fixed on those heavy stands of fir on the upper slopes and he smiled his mischievous smile.

It seemed like a thousand years ago, or just yesterday, when the Child was taken by his parents to the forest one late afternoon. The Black Forest appeared frightful and angry and restless and hungry. The Child saw a magnificent house almost hidden beyond the enormous trees. It stood tall and felt old and abandoned in the middle of the forest. As the trio walked against the fierce wind and flying leaves, candle light flickered inside to the rhythm of humming noises. *'Vril'* his father said. *'Vril'* his mother echoed. He didn't understand; he felt reluctance, slowing his pace but feeling the pull of

Order Out of Chaos

his parents' hands. *Did he dreamed this?* As they got closer the wind blew stronger, the dry leaves hit harsher against them and the humming became louder. Outside by the steps they waited. Was it the wind humming? The door seemed to opened itself, but out of the dark entrance a strange person wearing a blue hooded cloak bided them in. The humming was coming from there; and it wasn't a hum anymore, it was a strange language; it wasn't German though, nor a Germanic dialect, nor any known language, he was sure -by eleven years of age the Child fluently spoke four languages-, it was more like the great grandfather of the Latin.

Inside he was taken from his parents' hands by two other people also wearing blue hooded cloaks, with chains hanging from their necks with strange symbols and numbers. He suddenly felt calm, as if he had waited for this all his life. He closed his eyes and let the two cloaked men guide him to a foyer, where they undressed him with utter delicacy and rituality. The wind whistled through the cracks bringing the aroma of change.

His cellular phone rang in the background. He blinked out from memory lane -or dreamland- and reached for his inner pocket. Throughout the brief phone conversation he didn't speak a word, not even to answer the phone. His face turned sour and his eyes dimmed and narrowed; inhaled deep and held it. Then let go of it with dreaded disappointment. His jaw bones started dancing and the car turned freezing cold. 'Vladimir…'. He uttered, 'you poor soul…' He closed his eyes again, Damn you! He whispered within. The car kept rolling through, in dead silence.

In the main room, barely lit by the trembling candle light, a group of cloaked men stood in a semi-circle as if they've been waiting for him. They actually were. They've had waited many years for his coming. The only one wearing a black cloak stood in the middle and welcomed him. He asked him to step forward, and he did. His penetrating ice-blue eyes were the only visible feature under the hood. 'Do you know why you are standing here before us?' The Child nodded in confidence, and he didn't looked like a child anymore; his face had changed, it had a certain character that wasn't there before he came in. 'So bow before us, for you are about to be enlighten'. Without a thought he kneeled on the wooden floor that had the drawing of a pyramid with a wild staring eye at its cusp. 'You are about to see the truth, accept it and follow it'. He finished saying before they all surrounded him with their chanting and clicking. Their shadows kept enlarging and trembling as they got closer to him. All of them, about thirteen, put their hands on his head. He felt thirteen hands on his head at one time.

A red light swelled out of the fire place; he thought it was indeed fire, but this, whatever it was, had a certain translucence, a cold sensation, an unknown scent and it made him feel different somehow.

He was taken to another room, this one even darker than the other, and the black-cloaked one approached him with a book in one hand and a candle holder in the other. 'This is the book of life and death. Read it. You will find yourself, your meaning and your mission by the time you are done. Come out and tell us what it is that you have found'. And like that, the light from the candles extinguished. And so did he. Alone in the darkness he opened the book.

The meeting started at eleven-hundred hours. Although it had no official name, this meeting was known as The Round Table. It was composed by the heads of The Trilateral Commission and The Council of Foreign Relations, members of the Thought Society, Representatives of the House of Red Shield and the Council of Thirteen. There sat the unknown elite of the new world order. A decision-making body, the main source of international influence to governments and banks to media and corporations. The first topic of approach: The New Drug Reinforcement, Global Policy and Implementation.

The reason behind the relentless investment of time and influence and, most definitely, money into returning Vladimir Guzman to power in Peru, was the New Cocaine; The Breakfast of Gods. This new form of cocaine in its next evolutionary stage, had become the main choice for mass control in certain regions of the world. In Africa for example, it was distributed to the warlords of collapsed countries, they, in turn, would distribute it among the fighters who would become quickly addictive and extremely violent. Thus, their little wars would only end when the two sides have effectively killed each other. The New Cocaine was the main tool in the disposal of the weak, the dispensable; the cancer of the planet. The other side of it, as its other name 'the breakfast of gods' implied, was that for a different type of user, such as corporate executives, government officials, musicians, actors, and other artists, it was a new form of pleasurable addiction; with less hazardous side-effects and the ability to remain healthy, productive and oblivious, but most important, feel more powerful and focus, thus fueling the expansion of their reach. The drug had spread faster than estimated, hence its importance in the table of discussion. The need to establish more 'friendlier' governments throughout the world was a must, as well as new routes of distribution. Now that Vladimir Guzman had return to power, once again, the problem of production was taking cared of, Peru being the main producer of raw material.

And while the faceless and nameless discussed and proposed, Aesma Daeva thought of him; of such inappropriate time to do such foolish things, Vladimir! But he kept quiet listening to the arguments spoken by such prominent figures presenting alternatives to the issues at hand. This topic of approach lead directly to another one: The eradication, by all means possible, of independent traffickers of Drugs and Arms. And he couldn't help thinking of Vladimir again and his clandestine operation.

The great book resembled an antique bible, in its thickness and reverence, but he did not realized this until he finished it. He hadn't read it. He had stared at it, page after page, for it wasn't meant to be read, it was meant to be understood. The Child stepped out into the main room, where he found everyone standing, waiting in ceremonious silence. The flickering light was at its weakest then. The smell was neutral and the temperature was sleeping. He walked slowly towards the black-cloaked one; and as he approached, the circle began to enclose him again almost imperceptibly.

'Tell us who you are' The black-cloaked one said without opening his mouth.

'Aesma Daeva'. Replied the Child bathed in shadows.

'Tell us, what is your meaning'. The echoed voice came from behind and around and from the sides of the room.

'The alpha of the new Aeon'. He said with an angelic voice. They handed him a golden goblet covered in precious stones, and he drank from it.

'Vril is what you are, what you were, and always be, forevermore…' Is what he heard, he wasn't sure whom had said it, but that was irrelevant. 'From the beginning…we built the cities, we wrote the law, we guided the herd and spoke the word…Our Atlantean ancestors left us the heritage and the knowledge that we share with you now. You now belong to the Forgotten Race. Tell us, what is your mission' The just born Aesma Daeva lifted his head and looked - with ice-blue eyes- upwards and a strong wind blew through the room threatening the agonizing candle light.

'To lead the new age of world-government, the uniformation of land and people under the universal and eternal laws of Vril'.

The following topic of approach by the Round Table, proposed by Aesma Daeva, was the creation of the UIN or Universal Identification Number. A serial that would be issued by the government of

Order Out of Chaos

each country to its citizens and registered in an universal data base. The reason that would be given to the people was that in a world of mass Information-trading, less boundaries, and global interests, the Universal Identification Number will greatly improve services a given country can provide to a given individual at a given time, due to the fact that the individual's personal information and profile would be attainable by the local government from their terminals regardless the origin of the individual. Also, the new identification card will carry the scanned information of the individual's fingerprints, and fingerprints scanners will be installed everywhere, from airports to shops to banks and so on. So, for instance, in order for the individual to cash his or her paycheck, he or she will provide his UIN card and it will be scanned by the Bank Teller, at the same time, the individual will place his hand for his fingerprints to be scanned, if the information coincides he will receive his money; the same procedure would be used in airports, thus eliminating forgery, extra identification cards, passports, etc. The UIN card could also be used for purchases of any kind and it will certainly contain the individual's credit record, in case the individual decides to purchase a home or request a loan.

All of those in favor please raise your hands.

Gino Gianoli

Alexandria, Egypt

Never say never again: besides being the best James Bond movie ever, most importantly it became Timothy Moone's new favorite maxim. He kept whispering it to himself as this african heat suffocated him inside the tiny -european-make of course- shoe box of a car, speeding through *Horreya Avenue,* tilting from one side to another, as Bernard changed lanes constantly and unnecessarily. Oh yes, he was back alright; and somehow this city, this spit of land of white sands and magnificent scenery that stretches along the Mediterranean, hot and coastal, seemed to taunt him, to laugh at him.

And there it was, in Bernard's face, the repressed, and imminent sarcastic smile and I-told-you-so expression waiting to burst out of his face.

'Say it already!' Timothy said holding himself from falling down the steep slide of selfloathing.

'Okay, okay,' The Frenchman blurted out while smoking as the car swayed to the left again. 'So life is teaching you a lesson, so what?' The car swayed back to the mid-lane, horns were honking.

'What I don't understand is why am I coming with you to meet your contacts'.

Timothy Moone had arrived at midnight and headed straight to his hotel, where he slept straight through, and with no interruptions until noon the next day. The phone had rang and Bernard had told him to meet him down in the lobby, but to not bring the suitcase. Though it sounded strange to him, he did as told and now found himself in this shoebox sweating his ass out.

'It's just protocol, my friend, just protocol'.

'Well, this protocol better be fast'. He kept looking straight at the road. 'I'm in no mood to socialize anyway'. The car kept swaying and the heat kept rising and the wind wasn't blowing hard enough.

Bernard Bayard was a man that long ago had chosen to take the light side of things and not to take everything so serious; he was a joker with a razor sharp wit that didn't hesitate to use often. He also loved world history as much as women and cognac, and he enjoyed sharing this information with just about anyone who'd listen.

'I'm gonna teach you a history lesson my american cowboy,' He said with great excitement. Oh great! thought Timothy. 'This street we're riding on, is as old as Alexandria itself, during the time of Alexander, who you might have guessed, the city is named after, it was called Canoptic Street'. Bernard's head nodded in silence and to Timothy this was senseless, absurd, irrelevant, he wanted to scream: What the fuck?! And the French could see that, that his information wasn't being appreciated, in fact, it was being rejected and detested, but not ignored, which gave him the impression that he could continue. 'During the time of the Ptolemies, which some say was Alexandria's golden age...' Timothy who otherwise would've sit through and perhaps enjoyed a history lesson was in no mood for circumstantial superfluities that not only made him feel worse but had no relation whatsoever to his dreadful return.

So what would, the funny and knowledgeable, Bernard have told -or taught- Timothy about this small-great, sea city of many lives? First of all he would have gone off into one of his infamous pseudo-arias, and this one taken right out of Homer's Odyssey; he would've sang it loud, inside that shoebox-car, filling the claustrophobic interior with his cigarette breath:

Now off Egypt,
About as far as a ship can sail in a day
With a good stiff breeze behind her
There is an island called Pharos
It has a good harbour
From which vessels can get out into open sea
When they have taken in water

Then, acknowledging the confusion and, most likely, ignorance of the listener he would begin the tale:

Long before Alexander the Great passed through these lands, Homer wrote that paragraph -that was unjustly and unnecessarily made into a terrible song by Bernard- in his Odyssey. Of that harbor, only remains have been found off the island of Pharos, which is now the peninsula of Ras-El-Tin. Nothing of historical importance happened here until Alexander the Great arrived. He ordered a city be founded, and appointed the greek architect Dinocrates to build it to become Egypt's new capital. Alexander wouldn't see a single building rise, in fact, he would not see his beloved city ever again. His body was brought and buried here though, the exact location, still a mystery. After his death, all of Alexander's territories were divided among several rulers. Egypt was Ptolemy's piece of the pie. Under his rule, and of his successors (all first-named Ptolemy) Alexandria became the intellectual capital of the world and one of the first melting-pots in history: attracting such cultures as the Greek, Palestine, Jewish, Persian, and so on, until the last of the Ptolemaic rulers, a woman called Cleopatra, lost the famous battle of Actium and Egypt became a Roman province.

The Roman Empire didn't much care about Alexandria as a cultural center than a piece of land, its strategic location in the Mediterranean was its only true value to the Emperor Octavius. During the Roman occupation of Egypt, the world witnessed the birth of Christianity, and although its followers were persecuted, tortured and murdered by the thousands, it spread through the empire and its provinces, reaching Alexandria in no time. At first a few Christian centers spawned as the population grew slow but relentlessly, just like the persecutions where an astounding 144,000 martyrs were annihilated by Roman sword. Only when the Emperor Constantine announced Christianity as the official religion of the Empire the killings stopped. But as Christianity became the religion of choice, the priests, now with authoritative power, ordered the pagan temples to be closed down and their scriptures burnt. And in the meantime Alexandria saw the dawning of another change.

His name was Amr Ibn-el-'Aas and with him, Islam came to capture Alexandria. The Romans were loosing territories fast and their once-glorious empire was rapidly disintegrating. Without much effort the hordes of Islam inspired by their prophet Muhammed, took possession of Egypt and all northern Africa, reaching even Spain on the west; to the east the Muslim hand stretched as far as India.

Order Out of Chaos

So, Amr was appointed ruler of Egypt with Alexandria as its capital, as it had been for centuries. But there was a small problem: The Arab civilization was of land, not of water; they were horse riders not sailors, so they took an immediate dislike of the capital. And to add fuel to the fire there was a recurrent memory of Omar, the muslim Caliph: *'Establish you capital wherever you wish, but let there be no water between you and me'*. That did it. Alexandria couldn't be the capital. The Arabs moved east of the Nile, where they established another city, Al-Fostat, modern Cairo.

And so it goes that, for the next one thousand years or so, Alexandria would loose most, if not all, of its glamour and cultural heritage. It is said that many scrolls were burnt when, when asked what to do with them, the Caliph answered: 'If the knowledge found in them is contrary to the Koran, it is heresy, if it agrees with it, it it superfluous and repetitive, either way we don't need them'. The glorious Lighthouse fell, the Library was long gone, only some of the hundreds of theaters and monuments remained and the building of Mosques began. Then Napoleon came.

When Mr. Bounaparte rode through here with only 5000 men, he found no more that a small beach town, ready for the taking. The population was meager and the landscape deplorable. The French, needless to say, brought back some of Alexandria's own renown class and history, until the British (always the bloody British) decided that they wanted a piece too. What followed is however more confusing and boring to tell: The Ottomans had its share, the Mamelouks too, and between them they sucked Alexandria of the little it still had, whatever that was, until the British could not take this nonsense anymore and decided to bomb. This marked the beginning of British occupation of Alexandria, and Egypt that would last for 70 years. What happened in those long and boring years? Who cares.

Now, after all those foreign occupations, this city has a heart and personality of its own: its air, its people, its landscape is different from anywhere else in Egypt or in the world. It has a little of this and a little of that, a touch of Greek, a touch of Roman, British and French, a discrete splash of Christianity mixed with Paganism, and the definite impulse of Islam. And that is why, Bernard would finish saying, he wouldn't live anywhere else.

But he didn't. Instead he remained quiet and respected Timothy's inner turmoil, but he never stopped speeding.

They arrived to a run down building, east of Mansheya Square, where the pungent scent of old and cloistered ripped through their sinuses and shook their brains. As they climbed the squeaking stairs, the thought of the building being abandoned and perhaps uninhabited was becoming more and more plausible for Timothy Moone. On the third floor they stood in front of a door; archaic, cracked, and with character; the number 6 hung sideways clinging to the door by an agonizing screw; Timothy inspected it with a quick glance and thought of it as a cool background for a photograph, and after considering whether it should be black and white or color, with or without subjects, and if with subjects should it be a woman or a man, or both, or just him, or a thing, or maybe…Then he realized that Bernard hadn't even attempted to knock at it and as he was about to inquire why, the cracked old wooden door opened to a tall and slim man, wrapped in a black trenchcoat and hat covering half his forehead and covering his eyes with its shadow; an man of extremely white complexion, older, with strands of cherry-red hair crawling down his sides ending at his earlobes. He took a couple of steps out of the apartment, stood in front of them; now he was taller by a head; and without really looking in their eyes said in perfect and hyper-fast English:

'Let's go. Fifth landing. Be quiet. Strange individuals. All around us'. And as Timothy turned to Bernard in search of direction and explanation or, perhaps, translation; the frenchman had already started behind that strange looking individual. His contact name was Nicholas and the six-feet-something, slim monstrosity was wearing a long black trenchcoat and a hat that couldn't retain the stench coming from him. His eyes were as red as his hair and in the dimmed interior of this old building, they appear the more disturbing. In relative silence they reached to the fifth floor in spite the crackles of their footsteps on old wooden floor; they walked to the end of a filthy hallway and got into one of the apartments there. Traffic noise could be heard louder in there than outside: Horns, breaks, insults and interjections blended to create one endless intermittent sound; thick and confusing. Eventhough it was bright and sunny outside, in here it looked as if it was ten at night. It wasn't warm anymore, Timothy noticed, a strange thing since there was no airconditioning unit in sight anywhere. And to make the situation more eerie still, Nick, as he introduced himself, decided to put his sunglasses on, acquiring the look of an old undertaker.

'No time for banalities, gentlemen, so you will forgive my directness and bluntness'. A strange odor arose in the dark living room as they, Timothy and Bernard, were looking for a place to sit, deciding not to when not finding anything appropriate to sit on.

'Then, Nick, we won't waste much of your time, we want to know if your people would be interested in eleven kilos of 'breakfast' at three quarters of the regular price.' Bernard asked looking straight at him lighting and offering a cigarette. The other declined and leaned against what it seemed like an old armoire. His foot tapping.

'Eleven kilos of 'breakfast' is a lot of weigh'. Nick, the old undertaker-look-alike answered and Timothy didn't understand what the hell was happening there. Was that a joke? 'But the price is tempting'. He said.

Timothy Moone felt the whole thing a scam; there was something wrong here; first this enormous white clown with his mortuary outfit -that did *not* look the part of someone involved in this business, he actually resembled a latter day William Borroughs-, and now eleven kilos is a lot? twentyfive percent off? What were they talking about? The alarms in his head went off.

'We need the most discrete distribution within your circle, whoever you work with must not, can not and will not know beyond you, as the source of these, since we'll only be dealing with you'. Bernard's tone was serious and almost threatening, his hand was pointing while holding a cigarette. What the hell am I doing here? Timothy was thinking in the meantime.

'Tomorrow,' Nick replied. 'Pompey's Pillar, at two'. Without much of a nod, they headed out of the dark apartment leaving that white thing of a man standing there but before they closed the door he called out: 'You, with the blue hair'. Timothy stopped in his tracks and made a half turn.

'Yeah?'

'Do you know what being born with blue hair means?' After a few seconds, where he turned to Bernard and back he shrugged his shoulders.

'No, why don't you tell me'. Nick, the white undertaker-look-alike, took a step closer so that the only ray of light in the room would hit his face; taking the sunglasses off he said:

'Being born with blue hair means that you escaped your original fate,' He slowly moved his long and bony finger up and down, up and down. 'and that could be a good thing or a terrible one'. His eyes red, flickered invisible flames towards him. 'It all depends on the current fate that has befallen upon you, sometimes a better one, yes, other times...much, much worse, in any case it will have more significance, for good or for bad'.

That shook Timothy Moone for a split second, then he remembered he didn't believe in fate or destiny.

'I guess we'll just gonna have to wait and see won't we? Mr...'

'Nicholas' The other one helped him finish his sentence. 'But you can call me Old Nick'.

The door squeaked closed behind them and when they stepped out of the building the sunlight hit their eyes blinding them for a second.

On their way back to his hotel, Timothy had to ask Bernard about that…unusual -to say the least- meeting back there.

'What was unusual?' Replied a nonchalant Bernard, smoking and still driving fast. 'His look?' Timothy turned to him.

'Well, yes! don't you think so? He looked kinda freaky didn't he? but, that's not what I mean. What I mean is that thing of eleven kilos being a lot of weigh? What is that?' Bernard looked to him and back to the road, then back at him.

'You don't think eleven kilos of 'breakfast' is not a lot of weigh?' Looked back at the road and back at him again, his facial expression had dramatically changed, from this Timothy noticed that there was something he was missing, something he didn't know or worse yet, wasn't told.

'No…?' Timothy said and the car suddenly pulled to the side and the tires screeched, horns honked. Bernard pull the handbreak and reached towards him, and in a contained low voice he asked:

'Do you know what we are dealing with? Do you know about 'breakfast', ha? do you?' Timothy wasn't scare, he was worried, why did Vladimir Guzman put him up to this? How many times did he smuggled this 'breakfast' shit thinking all the time it was cocaine? How much more money are we talking about? Had he been used? Bernard sat back, fished out another cigarette and began cursing the air in French, then in Arabic.

Back in the warm silence of his hotel room, Timothy Moone couln't stop thinking about it. About what Bernard had told them on the way back: This new drug, what they called 'breakfast of gods', was the ultimate in purity, potency, and profit making: each kilo was worth, in Bernard's words: one million George Washingtons in this part of the world, and there were people ready to pay them, since that was the black market price sort-of-speak. The Organization had the monopoly of production and distribution and were charging as much as 1.5 to 2 million per package, per kilo. It was Vladimir Guzman's idea and creation of the side project where all profit would be divided into fifty percent for him, and twenty-five for each of them. The less involved, the larger the profit. In order for Vladimir Guzman to pull this out, he needed experienced people that worked for the Organization but weren't too attached to it. Bernard Bayard and Timothy Moone had worked with and for Vladimir Guzman on numerous occasions and were known to be as freelancers, sort-of-speak.

Timothy opened up the safe and took out a black leather suitcase where the eleven packets of this white powder laid, one after and in top of the other. With a fixed stare and a solid determination, he decided his fate.

The next morning he waited for Bernard in the lobby while reading the paper. A British newspaper reported in its headline the election of Vladimir Guzman to the presidency of his country, after a triumphal return, and quick elections. The article summarized 'the odyssey' Mr. Guzman had to go through, from the hiding in his friend's trunk to get to the airport, to his political exile and activity, to the murder of a presidential candidate and the famous video-tape of the now-imprisoned Ex-president Valverde, to his immediate return and successful five-week campaign. Timothy absentmindedly stared down at the front-page photograph of Vladimir: his mischief grind, one triumphal hand in the air throwing a V-sign, people surrounding him. The article ended with the announcement of an open-air public speech due to take place in two weeks in, a as of yet, undisclosed location. He put the paper down and saw Bernard approaching, the sun was lit and furious behind him, making him appear as a silhouette.

'Ready, Marlboro man?' He went for the bag but Timothy took it first. 'Quick at the draw ha, you *are* a cowboy'. He laughed his french laugh.

In the tiny car they headed to the meeting place.

'What is the Pompey's Pillar?' Asked Timothy.

Bernard, turning to him said:

'I don't know exactly when or why or who built it, but I do know that Pompey was Julius Caesar's nemesis and he followed him here to kill him, it is also him, Julius Caesar who is blamed for burning the Library'.

Timothy was looking out the window to the crowded *Mansheya Square*.

'You know cowboy,' Bernard started saying. 'There is a beach, one of the many public beaches here, called Miamy Beach?' He turned to him.

'Really?' Bernard lighting up a cigarette nodded.

'Yes, can you believe it? As an honor to your city'.

When they got out of the crowded streets into the more desolated ones, Timothy asked Bernard to pull over.

'Why? What is wrong cowboy?' Timothy had an expression of pain and nausea. 'Are you going to vomit cowboy?! Bernard screamed and the other one nodded. The car pulled to the side. Timothy opened his door and reached into his bag, and like a flash, pulled out his nine millimeter with the silencer attached and pointing at the Frenchman's forehead. His eyes widened and before he finished saying 'Merde!' a red splash flew out the opened window behind him, carrying pieces of his brain and skull. Smoke flowed out of both the gun and his forehead. Timothy wiped himself off taking all the time in the world, while cars flew on by, seldom and oblivious. He stepped out of the car and with a bag over his shoulder and the black suitcase in his hand, started walking along the road under the old and heavy Alexandrian sun and thrust by the immemorial Mediterranean breeze; he didn't look back.

As the plane flew over the vastness of the Atlantic, Timothy Moone rested his head on a pillow and his eyes shut, but he couldn't sleep. He knew there had to be consequences to what he'd done back there. What would Vladimir Guzman say when he finds out? What will he do? And right then his cellular phone vibrated in his shirt pocket. He was convinced it was Vladimir, somehow already informed of what had happened, and ready to sentence him to death. He decided, as the phone kept its incessant vibrations, that if he was going to die, he was going to die regardless whether he answered or not; so he answered.

'Hello?' A female voice answered.

'Mr, Moone, the wizard needs your attention'. His heart froze. 'The wizard needs your presence next thursday in room 606 of the Savoy Hotel in San Francisco, more details will be waiting for you in your mail'.

What would be waiting in his mail was a large manila envelope containing a plain ticket to San Francisco, his contact's name: Patricia Echevarria, another ticket to Lima, Peru, and information on his hotel, and money available. The contact waiting for him there would fill him in on details. Also, in addition to all of the above mentioned, the manila envelope contained photographs of his next Target: Vladimir Guzman.

In his dream Timothy couldn't sleep. He kept waking up: scare, sweating, trying to scream. Only by the fourth time of these rude awakenings did he realize that Francis hadn't been there, next to him in bed. A dreadful feeling overcame him: a feeling so thick and vivid he could've smell it. He tried to switch the bedside table lamp on, but it didn't: it was either unplugged or the bulb burnt. For a minute he wasn't really sure where he was, but as his eyes adjusted to the darkness he remembered and then he felt something wet. The bedsheets were wet on her side; he kept patting around it to assess just how big was the wet spot. Got up and tried to turn the bathroom lights on since its switch was closer than the bedroom's, but this one wouldn't turn on either; now he tried the bedroom's and nothing. 'Francis?'

He called weakly, standing at the door facing the bed. 'Francis?' This time he yelled. But no answer. Walking slowly in darkness and silence through the hallway, he tried the light there and also nothing; but it wasn't really silence; there was some kind of a humming noise, like wind blowing. He stepped into the living room and before he could try the switch there too, he saw the sliding doors leading to the balcony wide open, allowing a strong breeze to blow on the curtains keeping them flowing in the air and a few pieces of ornament, that were once arranged in a orderly manner on top of the coffee table, were now scattered all over the floor with magazines and their pages flapping back and forth violently. Was this another one of those strange dreams he'd been having lately? Did he really know where he was? He watched his step on his way to the balcony, and with the aid of the crystalline-blue moonlight, he discovered dark and wet tracks on the carpet, running beneath his feet, leading straight to the balcony in front and coming from around the hallway behind him. He hesitated. The ocean breeze carried the stench of foreboding. He followed the tracks towards the light and wind; the curtains flapped violently and the sense of nausea stretched itself awake. From the cushioning of the carpet to the coldness of the tile there was only one step; but what the sole of his bare foot felt instead, as he stepped out into the balcony, was something warm and thick, fluid and slippery. He had stepped into a puddle of god knows what. The previous stormy breeze fell still and silent, Timothy's eyes became colorblind and his ears soundproofed, all the while the dark fluid that was splashed all over the balcony's floor felt as thick and as sticky as a red wine demi glaze could get. With one foot on the balcony and the other still on the living room, holding himself to the sliding door, he kneeled in order to dip his finger in, to find out what the hell that fluid was by actually tasting it; and as his index and thumb rubbed one another to confirm the thick and sticky nature of the substance, followed by the tasting of it, the flash of blue and red lights were the first to break the spell. The color lights caught his attention first, then the noises: voices, radios, sirens…it was as if everything suddenly turned on, even the breeze switched violently on again. Everything came to him all at once. Slowly getting up, he finally stepped with both feet onto the wet balcony heading towards the veranda, leaned against it and look down to where all the commotion was coming from. He had to be dreaming, please, he had to be dreaming…The knocking at the door sounded too real though.

    Eleven stories down, in the kidney-shape pool floated the body of Francis, still wearing her babydoll, that used to be white but now was red, as the pool water, lighted and clear, now had a black stain oozing out, in slow motion, from the corpse and was inexorably spreading. The sounds at the door weren't knockings anymore, they were bangings and screams of 'open-up-now!'.

Like a zombie he stumbled back to the bedroom leaving a nice and red trail of footsteps on top of the previous tracks. As he tried to find his pants, still in darkness, the main door was bust opened and within five seconds he was on his belly, flashlights shooting all over the walls, floor, closets, bed, himself...radio voices speaking in numbers and codes. It was then when he saw the huge dark and wet spot on the bed, and the bloody trails of a body being dragged out of the bed, through the living room, into the the balcony, where it laid bleeding for a while, until it was dropped down, eleven stories down, to the pool. And there he laid: eyes wide open but not seeing, conscious but dreaming; handcuffed and kicked and yelled to and pulled and slapped, while in his mind he was thinking (or dreaming) about the woman in the white robe and her deep black eyes. Then he awoke to find himself in the hospital.

The cigar smoke had formed a cloud hovering above them. Darkness was the same but the few streaks of light had change direction. How long had she been there already? Minutes hours long? Hours days long? Too long, for her knees had numbed and her mouth had dried, again. Lara Walker knew what the policies were in a situation like this one, she had worked for the organization for quite sometime now and knew exactly what was going to happen next. She had stolen from them and she would certainly be punish. Baphomet stepped away, his voice an echo.

'Your situation, Ms. Walker, may I call you Lara?' She didn't answer, he wasn't expecting one either. 'As I was saying, your situation Lara, has turned into a problem, a big problem actually'. She closed her eyes and tried to mentally escape…anywhere, she didn't want to be aware as they'd put a bullet through her head. The situation had turned into a problem. He said, she heard. She tried to imagined something…faces flipped through her mind; Timothy again. Suddenly she felt guilt for what she did -even then it was more regret than guilt what was felt-, and for what she didn't do. She was mentally running, fast, faster, faster…Then a loud explosion with tenthousand echoes resounded in her ears, pierced through them to the rest of her body making it jerk once: a gun shot. She jumped on her numbed knees and popped open her eyes, saliva came and left her mouth again. The sound was still reverberating in her ears, in her brain, in her body; she got shot. Where? She didn't feel anything. Yet. Where's the pain? Gun smoke mixed with cigar smoke twirled around in a macabre dance across from her and realized that she wasn't going to be let off that fast. Once the smoke cleared off and her head stopped trembling she saw it: Eddie's face had ceased to be. It was his body laying there, contorted by the blow; those were his clothes soaked in blood…but…that wasn't his face. It wasn't a face. It was a dark smoking hole ringed with red overtones of protruding flesh, burnt hair, crushed bones and gunpowder all around it, expelling the putrid smell of post-mortem defecation.

Like he said, the situation had turned into a problem. She held her breath and closed her eyes again: Lima. Waking up and seeing Patty's face. A hangover softened by the scent of potpurry. In the shower. Hot water massaging her back. Soap foam. Patty joining her, naked. Staring. Not-thinking. Impulses. Kissing. Caressing. Looking some more. The death of reason. The triumph of the senses: Her hair caramel. Her eyes caramel. Her lips caramel. Her breast rubbing against hers. Their lips bounded by thirsty tongues. It felt good, sweet, exquisite. Refreshing, hot, cool. Clean, dirty, sexy. Her tanned body as slim as hers. Her eyes trembling; her mind lost. Thoughts as unnecessary as words. Warm water mixed with boiling saliva slithering down their mouths, chins, necks; fluid snakes of sex heading home; shoulders, breasts, tummies, and the snakes get closer, they race to the nest; hips and vulva, welcome home. In there, the water-saliva snakes mix with other fluids: they absorb, they feed and fatten the snakes that drip down their inner thighs...Remember? you could've died right there and then. Not here and now. But wait! don't leave this memory; not just yet. Where were you? Oh, right, yes, on your knees, licking, kissing, sucking...

After *the* quintessential shower, they left and headed to meet him. Yes, Timothy. The steakhouse, remember? and him sitting across you. His blue hair undone. His upperlip curled, his hands long and bony, his five o'clock shadow, his wrinkled shirt, his eyes kind and flirting, his voice tired and excited, his looks interested and a bit obsessive. Remember? you couldn't wait to see him the next day.

The voices had infested his brain and Timothy Moone found himself on the streets again somehow. He had been taken to the emergency room from Francis' place, but he had no recollection of it. How long was he in there? He didn't remember, and it didn't mattered anymore for the message was clear now: he had a mission, to speak the New Word and make the world follow the Word. The Word is of the one-God, his reemergence and revival; just like the old prophets before him, he'd been chosen to lead the way and establish a renewed relevance and impulse of the New Idea.

Was she interested to know what her problem was? The voice ripped through her eardrum and she was surprised to still be alive. A tear escaped out of her right eye out of impotence; not because her cousin laid there, with his face blown away and his brain matter and skull splinters splashed and scattered on the floor and walls, but because she should've known better, now her life was going to end like this? She wanted but couldn't mentally escape anymore, she tried, but everywhere she ran there were either mental locked doors or conscious dead ends. She fighted her eyelids to remain shut and not see the end, her brain to stop thinking about life and wondering about death, her ears to stop listening to the footsteps of inevitable doom. But what she heard instead was something her ears didn't expect, her brain wasn't ready for and her eyes had to see.

Her problem was that the merchandised was adultered, he said.

If she was breathing until then, she stopped right there and then. Did she hear what he just said?

Those eleven kilos of merchandise are eleven kilos of baby powder. She screamed a mute scream, the innermost of her soul shook and trembled. Now she was fucked. Her rational, her toughness, her experience, her shell, they all crumbled down now bearing the little child in search of her mother and cursing her father. Still, she had to say she didn't believed him eventhough he had no reason to lie.

'Oh no? You don't believe me?' With a slow but assuring step he walked to the rectangular table underneath the bright spotlight and picked one of the eleven packets on top of it; turned and walked right back in the same manner, calmly took a knife from god knows where and glided the sharp edge on the rubber surface, slicing it open. Held it up high and then poured its content all over her. The white avalanche was enough to cover her whole head and torso.

'Do you believe me now darling?'

She swallowed and choked and coughed baby powder. She was covered in white. She wanted the bullet right between her eyes, please, now. She didn't deserve to live after a fuck up of this magnitude, she thought and he said just that. Not only did she steal from the people that has taken care of her all these years, but she gets scam in the way, that's a double-fault.

What happened to you Lara? Pride was talking to her as she coughed curses and spat malediction. How did you let yourself get so low? She laid there on her side, her hands on her back cuffed and cheeks rubbing against the concrete. Why would you trade what you had for this? Clusters of saliva and tears mixed with powder stuck to her nose, chin and eyelids like miniature snowballs about to roll down the snow-covered mountain. Mrs. Karma had come to visit.

How does one spread the Word? Well, one must understand it and believe it first. In Timothy's case he believed alright, but he was yet to fully understand it. He attempted to speak, to release the clusters of words that accumulated at the tip of his tongue but he was afraid. What words would he hear coming out of his mouth? What would they sound like? What would they say? What would they command him? More and more questions brewed in that stormy mind of his only to be interrupted by intermittent thoughts and inner-visions of a world-to-come, but never, not even once, did he think about the past, his past: Francis, the restaurant, The Order, the killings, the trafficking, his frustrated attempts at being an artist...only the memory of that face, that translucent and feminine reflection remained hidden behind the retina of his mind as the sole survivor of his previous memory, his previous existence: Lara's face.

Lara Walker awoke, and wondered whether she was dead. For a second she was convinced she was since all she saw was darkness. A few minutes later she realized she was still alive: tied to a chair and blindfolded. She felt hungry all of the sudden. It felt like hours went by until she hear a noise: a door opening, steps, silence, breathing, more steps, a scent: tobacco; the same scent she smelled before. The blindfold was lifted off and her eyes hurt with light. She couldn't form an exact shape of the man in front of her, everything was still blury.

'You know Ms. Walker,' Said the voice of Baphomet. 'you are indeed a very pretty lady, and very deadly as they tell me'. Lara, as soon as her sight became operative once again wanted to ask how come wasn't she dead already, but somehow she couldn't formulate words, they were just dumb moans, it as if her mouth were numb. Her breathing became fast and her heart stomped as she tried again, mouth open, to utter her thoughts but only mongoloid sounds would come out.

'Oh by the way, we put a certain substance on your tongue that temporarily kills its nerves so you can actually feel how it is to not have a tongue'. She tried again with tears in her eyes.

Gino Gianoli

'Don't waste your energies, you'll be needing them soon for we have a mission for you'. Even her hysterical screams came out wrong, dumb, animalistic. She tried to break free from the plastic handcuffs that cut through her wrists, but it was useless, Baphomet in the meantime, snipped and burned the tip of his cigar with the utmost pleasure and patience.

Witzenhausen, Germany

A year prior to the meeting at the Luxembourg Gardens in Paris, Vladimir Guzman and Aesma Daeva met, along with others, in a large cottage-style house, in an area near the outskirts of the countryside of Berlin; where silence was worshiped, pure cool air was breathed, and vast green pastures were infinite. There, in an otherwise empty large living room, The Council of Thirteen plus Vladimir as a special guest, sat around the oval Lebanese cedar table to discuss the critical juncture where the current state of affairs of the Peruvian Government found itself.

The supposed crime-fighting government, led by President Ignacio Valverde, then in its third year in power, was up to their neck involved in bribery charges of officials of the Executive and Legislative branches, had total control of the Judiciary for self-benefit, and not only the continuation but the systematic increment of financial and logistical support of paramilitary death-squads; not to count the obligatory, implicit, collaboration with the drug trade. But of course, no evidence or witnesses were found to support these charges.

The Council was well aware that three years prior to this meeting, Vladimir Guzman himself was charged and indicted with some of those same charges, and consequently, had to flee the country in the midst of street protests and death threats. But that was the past and the populace has proved, time and time again, to have a short and selective memory.

The meeting was held to outline the first draft of Vladimir Guzman's return plan; where three strategic points were the main matter of focus: First, how the Valverde administration will be caught with their pants down, sort of speak, in illegal dealings, in a manner where the inculpatory evidence would be so explicit that would leave no place for doubts or denials. Second, how to prove Vladimir Guzman's innocence and political persecution, by the Valverde administration; and third -this one had Vladimir written all over it- how to accuse Ignacio Valverde of the much publicized, and still unsolved, murder of Presidential candidate Jose Carlos Echevarria a week before general elections.

You poor bastard. Thought Vladimir.

After nearly four hours of debates, plans, brainstorming and calculations -all in an international scale- the thirteen members and their special guest, stepped out into the courtyard where they were served, by three immaculate and professional butlers, fruit juices and assortment of pastries, along with some aperitifs and brandies.

They all seemed to enjoy their break as much as their meetings. These meetings took place once every three months in different locations; either different cities or countries.

Back in the board room, the next topic of approach, for which Vladimir Guzman could be no longer present, was the latest scandals involving the Russian President and his habitual use of the drug the German media was already calling: *Der Früshstück Der Götter.* Russia, a country torned and traumatized by the wrong Idea, had always been a symbolically important place for The Order. Many hundreds of years ago, members of The Order were persecuted throughout Europe by the Monarchs of the time, when they discovered that their days were numbered and plans were being made to disposed of them. The Church, then an important and powerful institution, advised the Monarchs against The Order, causing a continental-scale witch-hunt that consequently led to a massive exodus of Members to Russia and neighboring countries. Of course this part of History was never documented in the official books, but the fact is that a few years after the persecution, The Order invisibly took power in Russia and from there, it set out to rethink the strategies for the disintegration of the current world system.

But now, Russia found herself ruled by an unstable man that had once served a purpose and an idea, but had become erratic, unreliable, and of no longer use; in fact, he was a liability in a country too important to be indifferent to. The German Media had ran a report on the President's three-day-binges that included orgies, mayhem and once, even death. The continuous absenteeism by the President in world summits, government meetings and in his own executive office, was causing great concern in the military, whom, as told by German sources, were suspected of planning a military take over, a coup d'etat that could include the assassination of the President. That couldn't happen. A plan was unveiled to choose a young politician, strong and ambitious, to help him, with all the means necessary to become the next one to take over the rails. The plan was approved which meant the current President, had its days numbered.

Lima, Peru

In the baroque vastness of the Presidential Palace, Vladimir rehearsed the words and phrases, the shifting of tones: energetic highs and ambiguous lows; his body language: descriptive and eloquent, for his first public speech since his triumphal return. His reflected self seemed anxious and imposing in the life-size rococo mirror. It was going to be an outdoor speech, in front of hundreds, maybe thousands, of sympathizers and collaborators of some kind. Two months had flown by since his return and he had been only able to comment quick comments for the cameras, always coming and going, being taken and brought, surrounded by advisors, staff and bodyguards; there hadn't really been a chance to tell his version of the story, explain his immediate plans, or expose the circumstances in which the country, as a whole, found itself, nor, to promise the people what they had been promised before; what they wanted to be promised: hope. So that evening he would reconcile with his people, his country; together they would look forward and not back, and he would ask them if they were ready for a new beginning, and they would yell back a resounding YES! and he would say, admit, sell, state, scream, declare that *HE* is ready to lead the way. Were *THEY* ready to push through? A louder YES! would be heard across the country, not only in every home through TV cameras which would transmit this historical event live, commercial- free, but in the open air throughout the desert, mountains and jungle of Peru.

His return caused a great deal of political chit-chat, speculation, opposition and turmoil at homes, in TV and radio, in school, inside the country as well as outside. The vast majority however supported and celebrated his return, campaign and declaration as President. This time was definitely more exciting than the first one. A murdered presidential candidate and a deposed President later, Vladimir Guzman was ready to continue with his mission and the people were ready to embrace him.

Looking at himself in the mirror, glass of wine in one hand, loosed pages of text in another, he remembered how many times, as a child, he stood in front of another mirror, smaller and less pompous, at his grandfather's house; enacting, pretending, and performing as a would-be-President giving a nonsensical speech, with mannerisms and everything. His Grandfather, Juan Guzman, had been a politico himself, working in the low ends of some rightwing, by-now-extinct, political party, barely making ends meet, always hoping for his party and its leader to get to power; only then he'd have everything he wanted. Needless to say this never happened and at the worst time possible Agustin Guzman was born, forcing Juan to seek a more stable type of occupation, thus ending his feeble and hallucinatory political career.

Agustin, unlike his father hated politics, at first that is. He moved from Lima to the city of Arequipa were he would later meet Flor, a humble girl from peasant origins. As their courtship began to evolve from friendship to sexual to marital, Agustin's interests in current national affairs began also evolving from opinionative to activistic, but with a leftist mentality and inclination that would soon turn socialist, leading inevitably to communist. By this time his father had remarried, had a daughter, and divorced. No one knows who broke off with whom first: Agustin with his father or vice-versa. The fact is that he didn't have any contact with his father or halfsister, until one fateful day, old man Juan Guzman received a telegram from his unknown daughter-in-law, informing him of the death, years ago, of his only son. He had died of a shot in the back of his head and another one in his neck as he was supposedly trying to escape from a maximum security prison, with other political prisoners. It had happened more than ten years ago and only now was she breaking the promise she made to him. But he needed to know. The Prison's official explanation was of course false, ludicrous! in Flor's overdressed words. But Juan Guzman knew exactly why his son got sent to prison: In those years, a military government -not the first and one of the many to come afterwards- took power and immediately began persecuting members of the APRA (a socialist party that would later, conveniently, turn rightwinged) and Communists, declaring them outlaws and a threat to the stability of country. Agustin Guzman was apprehended, sentenced and jailed within two weeks. A month later he received a letter from Flor announcing her pregnancy. He knew that at least a communist regime would get to power, he was never going to see his son. (Did he know it was a boy? Of course he did. All men want a boy as their first child) So, it was either that or begin planning a revolt. Months later as the plan had gathered many supporters and was about to be executed, Agustin wrote a letter asking Flor to promise him two things: One, to name their son Vladimir, in honor to the man himself, the one that changed the world as they knew it: Vladimir Illich Lenin; two, if anything went wrong, not to let his father know about him, as far as he was concerned he was already dead to him anyway. That would be his final letter; his last words to her and his only legacy on him. A few days later he was rudely awaken, blindfolded and taken out of his cell with a handful of others, taken across a soccer dirt-field where, on their knees, they each received a shot in the back of their heads, followed by random blows. (one of them finding its way through his neck and into the dirt). The official statement we already know.

Months after receiving that dreadful telegram, Juan Guzman received Vladimir. He was twelve years of age and had travelled by himself, by bus mostly, from Arequipa to Lima, sent by his mother with the equivalent of ten american dollars -for travel expenses- to his grandfather's house in Lima. He would never see her again.

Vladimir would listen to bed-time political stories of revolution and oppression, the inevitable change would come, but it was taking too long. He grew up learning that wishing is only the first step, and one must not remain in it for too long or one would wind up like his grandpa: poor, lonely, obsolete…The one thing Juan Guzman did for his grandson was to enroll him in military academy before he died of hopelessness and cirrhosis.

Young Vladimir Guzman would prove to be an accelerated learner, of the intellectual kind, but with a touch of wit and impish impulses that later would developed into mischief fueled by the readings of Machiavelli's 'The Prince'. But his early vocation was completely military. He became Captain at the age of twentyone; making him the pride of the academy and the target of the envious. Soon he was working as the assistant of the Secretary of Defense. (Another military coup d'etat had taken place and a new Government promised reform). There he would meet a low-profile group of people, consisting of mostly Captains and Lieutenants, that called themselves: The Brotherhood. They all held key positions in the military and Government agencies. Vladimir would be welcomed into this secret society and his future would be determined.

Although all the members of The Brotherhood or *La Hermandad* got to where they were thanks to the current government, they were however highly critical and contemptuous of it, so far as to seeing it as a treasonous regime for its continuation of Communist persecution while engaging in secret million-dollar deals with the Soviets. Talks of another coup escaped from one's lips into another's ear, becoming louder and louder within La Hemandad's impermeable circle. Vladimir would teach them that wishing is only the first step and only those who are ready to lead, know how, or at least when, to turn that abstract wish into concrete reality. He took it to himself to take that second step. (it would be fair to say, however, that

Vladimir's wish was more of a opportunity-taking than an ideological one)

As a assistant to the Secretary of Defense, Col. Urruchaga, he had access to all kinds of classified documents that passed through his boss' desk. With the help of a contact, he sold those documents to the CIA, who was most interested in buying and requesting more information. The point was to give enough information and insight to the American Government about the dealings with the Soviets and the dangerous arms race in the region, to get enough support for a coup and money of course. This info-monetary trade went on for a whole year, detailing purchases all the way from bullets to jet-fighters. Somehow word permeated the impermeable brotherhood and one afternoon as he was leaving his office, Captain Vladimir Guzman was stopped, searched and arrested.

The military tribunal was ready to give him the death penalty for treason, but the Government wasn't ready to inform of one of his own, the military wunderkind, was going to be fussiladed. Not to count the national embarrassment this would cause. At the last minute the sentence was changed to life in prison without parole. Not a word of this got out to the public. Nor his escape to neighboring Ecuador or how the hell did he managed to do that. Some say he payed -with his CIA dollars- his way through, others say, La Hermandad influenced his way out of dodge.

For the next two years, Vladimir Gunman would jump from hideout to hideout in that tiny country, waiting for the fall of the Government. And a year later, it fell alright. Deposed by another military coup, promising reform as well, Vladimir Guzman saw it was time to return. Of course there was still a warrant on his head, so he had to pay his way back in, but as he arrived and was stepping out of the airport to smell that comforting air of home, he was detained and arrested and taken to jail. Apparently someone along the line, didn't get payed.

He was back home and in prison. He knew the new Government wasn't going to be as harsh with him and he also knew the way things worked around here. So, with what remained of his CIA dollars, he payed his lawyer -who happened to be his cousin-, and his sentence down from ten to five years.

In these obscure years Vladimir Guzman studied law with the help and under the tutelage of his cousin Romulo Guzman, who would later change his name to Rocoto Relleno. Romulo specialized in defending drug-traffickers and alikes, earning him an unscrupulous reputation, influential contacts and decent wealth. It was in this direction that Vladimir would be headed to. So, after five years, he would enter his cousin's firm, and in no time become the defense attorney of choice to the biggest drug-traffickers of the time. He no longer wished for money, now it was power. With enough cash and influential friends he ran for congress; getting elected at his first try. It was only then, as his new-found influence was being assimilated and becoming ever-hungrier, that La Hermandad got in contact with him again, there were higher mountains to climb. The same people plus a few others, again were holding key positions in the power structure of the country and again the word coup escaped someone's lips to inevitably land on Vladimir's fertile ears. But by this time the Brotherhood had grown so influential that it actively formed part of a larger world wide organization; and this was told to him: with their support, influential and financial, and a new idea of Government, this was very possible. Imminent, Vladimir thought. He would be chosen to lead once again. He now wished for the Presidency.

But first he would have to meet someone called Aesma Daeva.

The particulars of such meeting are obscure, but what we know is that a few years after it, Vladimir Guzman was chosen to run for his party, campaign for about eight months, and became the next President. At the party's headquarters, staff and supporters celebrated, members of La Hermandad were there too, everyone but the new leader of the country. Staring down from the penthouse balcony of Las Americas Hotel, Vladimir Guzman and Aesma Daeva puffed on Cohibas and sipped on Louis XIII.

'Now you must lead,' The mysterious man with ice-blue eyes said to him. 'You know that a new age is dawning upon us, and you to are play an active and important roll. But for now enjoy that delicious tasteless flavor of power'. In the following years Vladimir indulged indeed on power, blinding himself and making a series of inept and disastrous decisions that would cause him to flee his country, once again, and seek refuge in Paris.

But all that was forgotten, erased, conveniently blocked from people's consciousness. Now it was time for a new beginning, for change. With his glass of wine half full, and his tie too tight, Vladimir Guzman was constantly being circled by advisors, staff, campaigners and publicists like bees on a hive. He finished his wine and loosened his tie. It was time to go. It was time to talk to his people, his country.

Out of the Presidential Palace to a chilly and rancid night breeze into the official limousine, towards *El Agustino*, he comforted himself in the cushiony plush leather and alienating silence of the car's interior. He had agreed on the location for his inaugural speech with his publicists, for being popular, poor, and with a good lay out: the main plaza, where the stage was built, was surrounded by hills where the poorest of the poor had made their home by raising huts made out of straw material and adobe; these type of proto-homes sprouted all over, covering the hills in their entirety. The objective was that the people, wherever they stood, would have a good view of Vladimir Guzman, in what resembled a gigantic natural amphitheater.

And as the motorcade of limousine and police cars and patrol motorcycles, sirened their way through the colonial streets of downtown, to the more modern ones of the residential areas, to the dirtier and abandoned ones on the outerskirts, Vladimir Guzman felt content, invincible and ethereal; he felt a certain high that only one known drug could give. He inhaled once again and his mind heard: *'el desayuno de los dioses'* and this made him remember, it brought back a concern that had been put on hold: he should have received by now news from Bernard Bayard, the funny french as he called him, about the deal in Alexandria, where the crazy american, Mr. Moone, was also involved. But he'd have enough time to deal with this later, now, as the Americans would say, it was show time.

In the plaza, hundreds of people had gathered, mostly the habitants from the surrounding hills, they had come down to see Vladimir Guzman and to drink for free. Yes, there were two trucks parked in the corner, free beer and poster almanacs with Vladimir Guzman's face were handed down to the people, there were also t-shirts with his face and name printed on the front and with his slogan in the back: Order Out Of Chaos/ The Dawn of a New Beginning. A salsa orchestra began to play the hits, people started to dance and jump around, one great festivity had began.

After the they finished their set, the orchestra gave way to a man who stood in the balcony, -which was built as big as the stage next to it- where President Guzman would later stand, and began teaching the crowd chants and hymns and synchronized screams and applauses at his signal. He was the crowd warmer. Some of the people yelled insults back at him, telling him to get off, or jump, that they wanted more music and so, but at the end they all screamed and chanted along with him.

A soft and intermittent vibration was felt in the inner pocket of his blazer. Vladimir Guzman reached inside and fished out his cellular phone.

'Nervous, Mr. President?' The voice, far and familiar sounded too close and disturbing.

Order Out of Chaos

'Excited actually, this is it'. He replied.

'Yes, it certainly is. This night would go down in history my friend'. Aesma Daeva's voice was distant and foreboding.

'This night will be remembered as the night of change in the history books'. Vladimir added.

'Indeed it will be.' Answered the other. The limousine stopped and quickly, bodyguards and police personnel corded it around.

'Well, it's time to go, I guess you'll see everything on the television. Once again thank you and I'll be seeing you soon'. A bodyguard opened the door, the roar was heard.

'Yes, I will definitely see everything on the television. Vladimir, you deserve this, my friend, enjoy it and auf wiedersehen'. He stepped out and immediately was surrounded by guards and taken through a backstage and up a stairwell that lead to the balcony. The tidal roar of the crowd was increasingly louder and the energy in the air could not only be felt but be seen. The effects of the drug he inhaled were intensifying and he felt larger, stronger; he could see things no one else could. He wanted to speak, to scream, to feel their energy. And when the signal was given to him by the event coordinator, and to the people by the crowd warmer, he stepped onto the balcony under the bright spot lights, with the score from Strauss' 'Thus Spake

Zarathustra' playing through the speakers, and the crowd going berserk, jumping and screaming his name like fans in a rock concert.

A tidalwave of voices screaming his name, chanting 'The Dawn of a New Beginning' and 'we will triumph' and Vladimir taking it all in becoming bigger and stronger. He saw the sea of people and saw infinity and immortality, this is it, he quickly thought, this is where it all the steps lead to. How many steps did he take to get here? Did he remember the first one? The first wish? He wanted to let all those words accumulating in the tip of his tongue loose to invade the people's heart as his was being invaded by their roars. He moved forward to the ledge of the veranda and the roar became louder. He looked around him and saw staffers, advisors, leeches and tapeworms. He smiled his mischievous smile and turn to his people, then he felt something in his chest. An acute puncture in his thorax caused him to take one step back, making him teeter for a second. He regained his posture and tried to move forwards when another puncture, a few inches away from the first one, made him take several steps back; as he moved backwards a woman staffer lurched forward to support him holding his back and whispering in his ear *is there something wrong?* All this happening within three seconds, as she held him from moving backwards her face was witness being blown by a bullet. The explosion covered the left side of his face in blood and brain matter. As he reacted to the cracking sound, another bullet pierced his throat and he fell immediately after her. Only then did he realized that he'd been hit three times.

What followed was complete chaos. Chaos out of order: People stepping over him, screams, pushs and pulls; lights going off, cameras blocked; his blood dripping as he's dragged down the staircase, his life receding as he's thrown in the backseat of the official limousine. Darkness meddled with consciousness and feet began to feel cold, his bloody head, barely attached to his shoulders, rested on someone's lap. The last time he opened his eyes he saw, through the window, muted scenes of dirty streets and abandoned people.

Gino Gianoli

Vatican City, The Vatican

'...and what was the objective, in your opinion, of the art of the Renaissance my son?' Asked Bishop Valducci pointing at the ceiling of the Sistine Chapel to his honorable guest.

'Well...' Said the renown three-piece-suit man with ice-blue eyes. 'Personally, I believe that it was the re-awakening of the Human conscience; it somehow made mankind aware, once again, of their power to influence their own lives'. Answered Aesma Daeva standing beside the Bishop himself in the the heart of the navel. The two men had entered the Chapel with different agendas but the same appreciation for art.

'It is true, that mankind became once again conscious about himself and his place in the world,' Replied the elderly priest. 'but also in doing so, Man walked farther from God'. Both remained in holy silence for a little while, breathing stillness and absorbing colors. Michaelangelo's Adam and Eve, Saints and Angels, Snake and God, stared down at them...

'It is inevitable Father,' He broke the reverend silence with an enchanting voice. 'The Human condition is fueled by the quest for knowledge, by inquiring and searching for the answers'. Bishop

Valducci resumed his ninety year old step down the aisle sided by his guest. They moved slowly; their steps echoed.

'And that is also true my son, but that quest for answers sometimes makes us forget to live our lives and the people around us and most important of all, Him'. He pointed at the 15th century representation of God, mighty and busy, with the tip of his finger awakening Adam to life. There is movement and conviction in the painting.

Their stillness and contemplation were continuously interrupted by short intervals of snail-slow steps and a question-answer dialog.

The head of the Roman Catholic Church found himself indisposed to receive him today, due to a severe flu-like symptom affecting him; the Pope needed to rest. Father Valducci, the head Bishop of the Vatican, the number two as some called him, welcomed Aesma Daeva instead, and apologized for the inconvenience. Following a quick rundown of the agenda at hand and a light and tasty breakfast, Father Valducci invited him to a private walk into la Capella Sistina before they got down to business. Despite his ninety birthdays, slowness was only found in his movement, for the Bishop was a fast thinker and a cautious talker. His use of the Latin language was as fluent as his Italian and to his delight, it was matched with no effort by his guest; so they switched to that classical, efficient, yet dead idiom. And as they approached the majestic altar an inch at a time, the Bishop pulled out a set of large and antique keys to unlock the wooden doors leading to it. Sided by the wall paintings of Boticelli and Perugino they stood in pious stillness once again.

'I've always been fascinated with that story'. Pointed with his ice-blue eyes at the enormous and vivid Renaissance enactment of the Last Judgment. As a child that was the first story he memorized and imagined. He found it compelling and terrifying, absurd and inevitable. He had pictured it in many different styles and ways; but this one in front of him was the quintessential portrayal of the rewarding of the just, rising of the dead and falling of the damned.

'Many people have taken for it granted.' The ancestral voice of Bishop Valducci carried lamentation and understanding 'People think of it as no more than a fairy tale.' Aesma Daeva's eyes narrowed and focused on the painted Judge: Jesus, condemning, rewarding, choosing, pointing, looking down, rising, floating, omnipotent, God.

'In a certain way it is, don't you think Father.' He declared. 'Just as the story of Creation, it was meant to be a fable with a moral undertone, no more than that'. The bishop drew a peaceful smile as if he had heard this comment a thousand times before.

'The people who told these stories, or…fables, did not pretend to foretell the future or retell the past as it was, instead, they were wise enough to foresee what was to become of men in its tireless quest for knowledge: his own damnation and destruction; and to tell the past in a simple but accurate manner for the people of that time to comprehend'. Said the Bishop and now it was Aesma Daeva's turn to draw a smile on his face. Standing a few steps behind, the Bishop saw how his guest's anatomy blended into the enormous and colorful and enveloping painting in front of them, and if we had stood behind the Bishop, we would've seen how his black and red attire made him stand out. 'So,' the bishop began to speak again, 'if you don't mind me asking, what is your business with the Pious XII documents?' The back of Aesma Daeva seemed square and solid, like a hologram coming out of the painting.

The truth was that there was an special interest in the afore mentioned documents by the Council of Thirteen, for they contained data regarding then-Pope Pious XII supposed oblivion to the mass murders of Jews by the Nazis; and the absent protest, or even comment, from the Vatican Pontiff. Needless to say, the Vatican itself have denied such indifference from the former representative of Jesus on earth, stating that he actually did everything he could within his powers, once the nefarious news surfaced, to raise ethical and moral questions about the motive and procedure the Nazis applied to expel, or shall we say, cleanse, Germany from the jewish influence. Indeed it was suspected that these documents, kept under lock and key in the Vatican vaults ever since, would shed light on the role the Roman Catholic Church played, or consciously decided not to play, in the obscure years of the second big war. So, after years of international pressure and to avoid world-wide embarrassing speculation, the Holy Church decided to allow a gradual disclosure of the documents, meaning the opening and examination of one document at a time per year, to a selected group of people; including religious scholars, historians and certain emissaries from the United Nations, hence, Aesma Daeva's presence here. To Father Valducci the interest of scholars and historians in these documents was obvious, but his guest, though knowledgeable and well researched, was neither nor; and this was his quiet concern.

It would be fair to say that a slight chill was suddenly felt in the chapel. Taking another millimetrical step forward, Father Valducci got closer to him, as if to hear better what he had to say.

'I thought we were going to get to our agenda later on tonight Father'. He answered with a certain mischievous nonchalance to a suspicious and disappointed Bishop. Aesma Daeva turned back to face the Altar painting of the Last Judgment making the Bishop wonder.

'Tell me then, what do you see in there?' The mural in its exuberance in color and magnitude in illustration showed the heavens above opening with heavenly light shining, with angels descending, some to lift the chosen ones, some to push the damned downwards; Then there's the Judge, Jesus, beneath him souls crying, suffering, falling, pleading...then the demons taking, devouring, indulging...hell in the bottom, in the end. The scene begins with light blues and soothing whites at the top, that gradually turn into hot oranges and burning reds as they descend.

'What I see,' He replied. 'I see the last great era of religion, as the engine of morality and art; well, to tell the truth, the Church, by the time Signiori Bounarotti began painting this mural, had long lost its vanguardism in the morality area, no offense; but was however the main propeller of the Rennaisance art movement, eventhough art ceased having God, Jesus or saints as their main characters but Man himself. Individuality was reborn. So, what we have here in front of us, Father, is the last great contribution of religion to humanity: paid art.' The Bishop let a series of incredulous laughs that ended with some coughs.

'Well...I must tell you,' he said clearing his throat. 'I have never thought of it that way, nevertheless, you have a point'.

They turned together and began to walk back, through the wooden doors, leaving the altar behind them, to the middle of heart of the chapel where we first encountered both personalities. Sided by papal portraits and saintly compositions they each enjoyed that particular moment from different perspectives: One by the abundance of art representative of a time of change, a time when Man reborn himself and broke with the old thinking and traditions; the other by being the fortunate host and guide to this magnificent storage of human art form derived from divine inspiration.

'Just remember,' The Bishop restarted. 'To believe in a god or gods is as innate in the human species just like, or more powerful than, its quest for knowing; for it is the belief in something that really propels the human species forward'. The painted saintly papal portraits seemed to agree with him in silence and to be giving a certain look of scorn directed to his guest.

'I am of the opinion,' He replied. 'that it is *necessity* that which propels the human spirit; the necessity to know, the necessity to see beyond our skies and oceans, the necessity to feel. Every time a scientist makes a breakthrough discovery, an artist pushes the boundaries of vision and feelings, or a thinker revolutionizes the current thought, humanity in general take a step forward; it evolves as a whole; and it is *Belief*, that what bounds humanity to the ground; beliefs causes the mind to stop inquiring; to stop thinking'. Now, even the 17th century frescoed-God floating above them forgot about Adam and stared directly down at him.

'My son,' Replied the Bishop. 'once you've reach my age you'll know just how important belief is in one's life. Without belief there is only the dark and cold abyss. So at the end of the road one must choose: either to belief in nothing and forever be in search of knowledge, that will only show one, time and time again, how small and insignificant one is, or, one chooses to believe in something more powerful and divine than one's self and the *promise* of a better existence beyond death, the *promise* of a reason behind all this. Don't forget my son, knowledge doesn't necessarily mean wisdom'.

'The Promise?' Counter attacked Aesma Daeva. 'The promise from whom? From a God that has long ago abandoned its supposed beloved children? That made Man turn on each other for his sake?' The Bishop quickly interjected.

'No! You are wrong. God didn't make Man turn on each other, Man himself did in the name of his own God'.

'I beg your pardon Father,' Answered him. 'but it has been the same one God that has been manifesting in different disguises to different people to the point of promising the same land to the Jews, Moslems and Christians, he should have supposed, at least suspected, that that would've, and indeed did, cause trouble -and I'm using the word 'trouble' loosely'.

Once again silence took over the two men and the chapel. Then they started walking towards the main doors.

'It is sad,' The Bishop softly said, as if he was talking to himself. 'to hear that since we ran out of people to point our fingers to, we now blame God for our transgressions'. Aesma Daeva in the same low tone of voice responded:

'Once again Father, I beg your pardon but, if God really created us, then he should take part on the blame, since we are *his* creation. Maybe, who knows, he is like Dr.Frankenstein who gave life to this being who first would obey all his commands, but then one day it became aware of itself, of what it was, and rebelled against him, to later kill him'.

'That was a monster, if I'm not mistaking, I would hate to compare Mankind to that'.

'Perhaps Father, us too are monsters in our own right. God created us, ignorant and pure creatures, then we grew and became aware of ourselves, of the world, of cruelty and evil and the harm that we pose to ourselves as beings, and we realize that it is not all our fault, the world is like this; so we question God for it. Then when no satisfactory answer is given, we begin to hate him, for creating and placing us in a world so dirty and corrupted; then we begin to realize that the only way out is to kill him, to liberate ourselves, to take our souls back. And here we are Father, talking about it. And the irony of it all is, that the same people who were place to keep his legacy, to keep reminding us about his mercy and his wrath, are the same people who hold the dagger that we'll use'. The Bishop wanted to blurt something but Aesma Daeva continued and his voice had change: more ethereal, infecting and ancient.

'And we knew this was inevitable, it was bound to happen, so you prepared your people for it, for the times to come, for the times that we live in. But you changed the story completely, like you have so many times before, by creating this character, this ultimate villain: The Antichrist, who would come and seduce the world and enslave humanity'.

The Bishop's gaze seemed transfixed into nothingness as if Aesma Daeva were speaking to someone inside the Bishop's body.

'But we know the truth, don't we old friend. Your reign will soon be over and the shackles which have held Mankind bounded to the ground are fast becoming rusted and weak. Our liberator, knowledge: your Antichrist, is here, and the truth is quickly spreading; Man will soon see a new beginning, a new world order, free from your chains of guilt and remorse, where the weak and their diseases will be eradicated'.

An hour later both men were seen coming out of the Sistine Chapel supposedly engaged in a friendly, if not amusing, conversation. Then they boarded a limousine and headed to the Vatican's main offices where a very selected group of scholars were to meet them in regard of the Pope Pious XII's documents.

Months later, the news of the documents and declassified information would leak to the media worldwide, bringing much and devastating criticism to the Roman Catholic Church and to its leaders; raising questions of relevance and morality. About two weeks before the news about the Documents broke loose, Bishop Valducci was found dead in his bed. A stroke was determined as the cause of death.

An interesting fact is that on his night table his journal was found open to the last page where he had written: *"Father, I know not where I am heading to, but after my encounter with your favorite angel, and the torturous months that followed, I think I rather not know. Why have you lied to us?"*

Gino Gianoli

Under medicated submission, Lara was allowed to sit at one end of the dinner table. Her eyes seemed tired and her attitude beaten to the ground, she wore clean clothes and her hair had been badly cut short; 'chopped' would be the word she'd use. A plate of vegetables was served in front of her, and she felt just like that. At the other end, Baphomet, the only other person in the gigantic dining room, sat staring at her through four silver candle holders carefully placed along the center of the large table; right in front of him rested a file containing papers and photographs. She realized she also had a file in front of her, next to her plate. Without saying a word she opened it to find a photograph of Timothy Moone. Her expression twitched.

'There you will find everything you need to know, my dear. That's your new and final Target. If you are successful, which I trust you will be, your life will be spare and you may go about your life and never hear from us again'. He sighed. 'If you're not, well…need I waste my words? Go on dear, get out of here. Find him and kill him'. She got up and walked on shaky legs out of the large and dark dining room. Before she realized what had happened and what she held in her hands, she was on a ferry out of Fisher Island.

Her face had changed: her abysmally-black eyes seemed shallow and dull, her long hair chopped short and its blackness faded into a dark rat-grey, her semblance mistreated and in need of rest made her seem twenty years older, her lips no longer curled like a rose nor stretched from cheek to cheek, for they lacked blood circulation and reasons to smile. She had also lost significant weigh and almost fully regained the nerves of her tongue.

She pulled herself to a dingy motel, by the airport. Flipping through papers of information and photographs of Timothy, there was a slight nostalgic reminiscense in her tortured expression as she went through the file, that could be interpreted two ways: one, a certain sentimentality about her former job, where she had been one of the best and had felt part of an important cause, even when she didn't really know what 'the cause' was; and two, because, as opposed to Timothy, she did remember him vividly, not like some abstract human figure with a hidden meaning, but a real being in her recent memory with many mixed feelings attached to it. It had been still less than a month since she last saw him at The Lowes.

The intense heat of June makes one see things sometimes. To Timothy Moone, it made him not only see but hear things as well. He had, somehow, managed to cross the 41st street Causeway into Biscayne Boulevard. He kept going straight, further into Downtown. As the landscape became dirtier and threatening, the voices turned clear and soothing: they flowed like rivers of revelation, dripping its guidance and reassurance into his heart. And even when the sun had given up its ultraviolet whipping and darkness began to surround him, he felt at ease with the world, cool in his head and purposeful in his walk. 'The world needs to change'. He whispered to himself.

Hours later hunger struck and now the noises originated in his gut. Without thinking twice he headed into a dark alley towards the dumpsters. The stench was strong but hunger was stronger; he jumped into the once-green, now-rusted and corroded dumpster and began its meticulous selection of would-be-dinner items. Oh how delicious would be to have in his mouth the velvety texture and melting orgasm of seared foie gras swimming in apple chutney. Had he forgotten about that too? Perhaps, perhaps not, but for now, hard and cold residues of a bagel, a blackened banana and several pieces of pizza crust would have to do. As he jumped out of the dumpster with dinner-thoughts in his head and saliva rushing -in a quintessential Pavlovian fashion- in his mouth, he felt a thump in the back of his head and suddenly found himself on the pavement; screaming voices -these ones definitely weren't in his head- and kicks followed. He never saw the three derelicts approaching from behind, whom for years have claimed this alley as their home, their territory and were determined to teach him the consequences of trespassing and stealing their food. As one swung the flat wooden board against his shoulders, and the other kicked him in the ribs twice and landed one in the face, the third one yelled, in a raspy, alcohol-deteriorated voice, words that only he could understand. Right there and then Timothy Moone saw his end. 'Not like this, not here' his mind said. Actually he had escaped into his mind, he wasn't feeling anymore pain, although his body was being trampled and beaten, kicked and dragged. Suddenly it stopped; the screams, the beating; the derelicts fell silent and proceeded to run away, stumbling with each other. That's when he realized he was back into his body, and the pain was real, acute and ubiquitous. Lying on the filthy cement, in puddles of mud and piss, he thought he saw someone standing in the corner, he closed his eyes and thought about his childhood: sitting at home watching cartoons, doing his homework, eating his favorite sandwich...then, he heard him approaching; he tried to see him but he could only hear his steps in that dark, filthy and desolated alley.

The first question that crossed Lara's head was: Is he still here? According to the information provided by the file, the answer was yes. The match of his description had been seen in Miami Beach in the last two weeks and according to witness testimony, he looked dazed and lost, beaten and with no orientation or direction. To Lara, this information made no sense. The last time she saw him he was...he was insane, he wanted to runaway with her; he loved her! he said for christ's sake, and then...and then brought that damn suitcase. The minute she saw it she knew it meant trouble. However he came into possession of it, it couldn't have been good, in fact it was dangerous, or worse yet, deadly. She knew, goddamnit, she knew! Lying on that cheap bed that god knows how many people have fucked on, she felt too tire to cry; too tire to regret.

It was his way out, he said, the suitcase and her were his future. Of course she objected, she didn't feel the same about him, or did she? In any case, he, by stealing the suitcase and bringing it to her hotel room, had become a liability for her, in fact she was already in trouble; it would be a matter of time until they get to him and by default her. In that moment, in that eternal second, the thought of taking him out herself and returning the suitcase, didn't just crossed her mind, it walked in circles, it came and went, it lingered there in her head, lounging, taking its time, enjoying the wait. Then came the phonecall and he had to go, leaving the suitcase at her disposal. She changed and took off with it, hoping that the trail for the case would end with Timothy. So what happened to him? He's supposed to have been dead for more than a month now, why did they take so long?

What Lara Walker didn't know it's that they did caught up with Timothy the same day she left the hotel, and indeed was supposed to be dead, for he *was* left for dead in the ocean, only to end up, miraculously, waking up in the shores of South Beach last Sunday.

So, if he's here, where could he be? Lara closed her tired eyes and tried to think like Timothy.

Not even Timothy knew where he was. He regained consciousness after one of his inner-voices kept whispering the word *'fellowship'* for the millionth time. He saw a fireplace but no fire. It was dark and humid; the open window had let a blitzkrieg of mosquitoes in and the only light available was good old moonlight. Then he realized the window wasn't open for there was no window, just a square whole in the wall; the entrance or exit of the room where he was had also just a frame, no door. He found himself lying on some kind of thin mattress infested with patches and stains, in such a decaying condition that some rusted springs had busted through the colorless fabric. He also felt and counted the fresh bandages in his forehead and arms, being six in total; then noticed himself in underwear and with an overwhelming hunger, only comparable to the astonishing thirst of the mammoth mosquitoes sucking on his neck.

'If you command them not to bite you they will leave you alone'. Said a voice coming from a silhouette of a man, standing at the doorless archway.

'Who are you?' Asked Timothy again crushing a couple more mosquitoes on his shoulder. The darkened man stepped forward and let the feeble moonlight fall upon him. He was holding a tray.

'Hello, my name is Babeuf, and this is my home'. He placed the tray on one end of the cot, there, Timothy saw food: two bananas, a bowl of what seemed to be oat meal and bread.

'Here, you must be famished'. Without a second of hesitation he proceeded to stuff his mouth. 'Whenever you feel better,' Babeuf said while Timothy chewed and swallowed. 'I would like you to meet our family'. With that said he walked away, leaving the beaten guest bent over the tray of food, eating with both his hands.

It only took a couple of phone calls for her to find out where the restaurant was located. Lara had dyed her chopped hair blonde giving her an early 80's punk-new wave look. With dark sunglasses and a pin-stripe, dark-blue suit -that would've seen more appropriate on a woman-CEO -, she headed out into the scorching heat and thick humidity to hunt Timothy Moone down.

The restaurant had opened for lunch a couple of hours before and since there were only three tables, Serge, a server now, was standing by the hostess stand staring out into Ocean Drive thinking how hard is to make any money in the summertime. The streets keep bustling with people who pass by and sometimes take a peak at the menu but only a few of them actually decide to come in. He was thinking -

and suffering with the thought- about the amount of 'doubles' he was going to have to work this week, when a tall and slim woman, spiked blonde, and professional looking, requested to speak with the manager. Francis, ever devoted to the restaurant, had to stop the inventory paper work to come out and attend to this funky looking lady who she would later describe as an Executive Cindy Lauper.

After introducing herself as a private detective, named Alicia Rommel, hired by the Moone family, Lara asked Francis for a couple of minutes of her time. In the furthest table, by the corner, the two women sat facing each other, one holding a briefcase, the other offering something to drink. Lara, or Alicia, began recounting the supposed pleading by Timothy Moone's parents to know about his son's whereabouts since no one had heard anything from him in months. Francis had never heard anything about Timothy's parents, then again, she did know little about him. Lara, proceeded to ask some preliminary questions and Francis told her about how Serge had found him in the back alley by the dumpster; that had occurred about…almost a week ago, last Sunday.

'What was his condition?' Asked Lara.

'Horrible. He…he looked so…' Francis had to sip some of her water. Then continue relating how she took him to her condo, that same night, and how he had trouble remembering who he was and who *she* was, and the restaurant and…his whole life. She told her with great pain how he seemed to had no idea of what happened to him or where he'd been for the last month and everything that followed. 'He just seem…crazy you know'.

'How so?' Lara started taking notes.

'He just, talked incoherence, you know, nonsense, about voices and…'

'Voices, what kind of voices?'

'I really don't know what to tell you Ms. Rommel'.

'Please call me Alicia, I'm not that old'. Francis took a deep sigh and a sip of water then she paused.

'He would, have these spasms, like epilepsy you know, and he…he would scream. Oh it was horrible I tell you. He was another person, unrecognizable'. They remained in silence for a little while; Lara imagining, Francis remembering.

'So you take care of the restaurant now?' Lara broke the spell.

'Well someone has to, I mean, it still belongs to Timothy and I will continue to run it until they tell me otherwise'.

'Who are they?'

'His family. I'm sure they want something to do with this business, isn't that why you're here?' A couple were sat and greeted by Serge in the table by the window. Francis was looking at them but wasn't really seeing, she seemed to be tired, despaired, disappointed.

'No, that's not why I'm here,' She heard the pseudo-detective say. 'They are just interested in their son's whereabouts, that's all'.

'Well, I am very interested as well, believe me, he's a very dear person to me'.

Lara asked her if anything strange had happened since his disappearance.

'No, not really…wait, about a month ago, about the same time Timothy was supposed to be back, someone broke into the restaurant and managed to open up the safes'.

'They didn't take anything?'

'No, they just went through the office and turned it upside down, both safes were empty'.

Francis finished by telling her how devastated she was when she went to visit Timothy at the hospital, the day after rescue took him after one of his fits. She should've stayed there, beside him, she said but the hospital personnel didn't allowed her to.

'He was just gone, no one knew anything, can you believe it? He just got up and waltzed right out of there, incredible isn't it?' Lara just managed to nod her blonde spiky mop.

'When did this happened?'

'Three days ago'.

As Lara Walker walked out of the restaurant leaving Francis Green more confused and lonely, Timothy Moone was dreaming about two women. These women were following him, naked and beaten, through an endless dirt road sided by desert dunes on one side and a filthy river on the other. Then he realized that the two women were bounded by their necks and feet with long rusted chains which he used to drag them behind him; the women pleaded for forgiveness and Timothy, with whip in hand, felt hot, sweaty and sticky. And like this: hot, sweaty and sticky, he awoke. Through the whole in the wall the sun rays illuminated and heated the otherwise empty room; a tray with food residues laid around and he remembered: the mosquitoes, the man, the food. The room itself looked abandoned and dirty; its humid peeling walls had yellowish and brownish spots like some kind of disease, the floor, once hardwood, was opaque and rotten by generations of termites. In the corner stood a fireplace that had been repainted time and time again, making its details hard to distinguish. It was when he was trying to figure this out when he heard chants and synchronized claps coming from outside. Once he started limping he became aware of his bruises and aches, and that he was on a second floor. Holding on to a rusted metal rail he began his odyssey down the stairs as the chants and singing became louder and softer at the same time. The bandages on his forehead were slipping off because of the amount of sweat, due to the heat and the effort it took not to fall. When he conquered the first flight of stairs he leaned against the wall to rest, then he continued.

In what would be the living room of the house, a congregation of women, children and men sat in a circle, singing along the lines from a booklet each held in their hands. When he saw this and stopped coming down, everyone ceased to sing and turned to him.

'Please come down and join us'. Said who appeared to be the oldest and leader in the group, who was young himself.

'Oh, please don't stop for me,' A confused and aching Timothy said. 'it will take me a while to go down the rest of the stairs'. No one made a comment nor a movement, there was a certain awe in their gaze.

'Then we shall wait'. Said the young man.

Order Out of Chaos

Lima, Peru

Along with millions of shocked viewers and weeping televiewers, Anais and Patty Echevarria saw the live assassination, commercial-free, of President Guzman -Dallas 1963 came to mind but with no Oswald. Phones started ringing off the hook at the Echevarria's residence; ground and mobile lines gave off its various tones and harmonies at a synchronized go. Patty quickly walked to the kitchen with phone on her ear and a relaxed step, while her mother, the Senator, with wild open eyes and trembling hands, tried to answer both house lines while searching in her purse for the wireless one.

Talks of a military junta plotting a coup sprouted all over the country like itchy body eruptions caused by a bad rash. The frightened higher class prepared its luggage for departure as the lower ones awaited for yet another round of ritualistic promises and inevitable chaos. Cynicism and despair became the national anthems while the power circles struggled to take ahold of the much tainted Presidential Seat. No one in the whole country knew what was going to happen next; some actually wanted the military to take control of the decaying political situation. For over twenty years now, the military hadn't been in power; the ever expanding and influential air of democracy had been reason enough to let civilians govern the country; but with all these national chaos and televised murders people were beginning to wonder about the fragility and corruptionality of latter governments. But on the other side of the world, across the Atlantic, it had already been decided who would be the next President.

It had been a little over four years since her husband, Jose Carlos Echevarria, was murdered in cold blood that fateful morning when he went to grab some milk and other groceries. The wound hadn't healed yet, memories were still vividly clear, voices were still being spoken in her head and that last kiss, he gave her in the kitchen before he stepped out, was still felt in her lips. The televised assassination of Vladimir Guzman only made the wound boil and memories stirred violently in her heart -for those kind of memories are not stored in one's head, they remain in the heart. And her heart remembered alright. It still recalled that overcast and drizzling morning: she had turned the news on, on the tiny television set in the kitchen. She sat reading the paper and listening to the morning news. The news anchor spoke about the whereabouts of Vladimir Guzman and the way he managed to flee the country -an special emphasis was made at the fact that he had to hide in the trunk of a friend's car. The maid, as she cleaned the countertop, realizing how long Mr. Jose Carlos was taking, commented it to Mrs. Anais. She took a look at the kitchen clock and in fact, twenty-five minutes had passed by when it should've been ten. She dialed his cellular phone and waited for an answer. As she waited for him to pick up, the second line began to ring and the maid answered: 'It's the police Señora, something happened'. Two minutes later she was storming out of the house, with tears in her eyes and a knot in her throat, to the patrol car outside.

They arrived to the scene of the crime as the TV stations vans lifted their micro-wave antennas and released their batallion of reporters and cameras-this would be her first encounter with the Media. What she saw she'd rather not remember but it is always there: swarms of people and much noise, around a body half-covered with newspapers that kept flying away and exposing his contorted body, his opened mouth, blood-stained face and huge crater, dark-red, in his forehead. Next thing she remembers was waking up in her bed, she had passed out from the shock, and asking to get ahold of Patty, she didn't know what or how she was going to tell her what had happened to her father, she didn't even know how to tell *herself* what had happened to her husband.

By the time Patty received the news from her mother about her father's tragedy, she found herself alone in the city of Cuzco where she was scheduled for a four-day trek up to the Inca ruins of Macchu Picchu. That afternoon the rain poured down in Cuzco but only drizzled in Lima; as always.

People were beginning to speculate about a curse in the Presidential Seat and one could easily understand why: Jose Carlos Echvarria who the polls and the people on the street had pre-determined to become the next President was found dead on the pavement; assassinated. Ignacio Valverde, the one who became President by default, was residing now in a maximum security Prison on charges of Corruption, Abuse of Authority, Obstruction of Justice and Murder. Now the much expected and talked about kiss-and-make-up between Vladimir Guzman and the people, was cut short by three bullets, on national television. Anais, after the initial shock, was heard saying how dangerous has turn out to be President in this country.

Three weeks later all eyes were on her. Suddenly there was a rumor on the streets that she, Mrs. Echevarria, will run for president. The loud secret was the topic of the month, maybe of the year, discussed in taxi cabs, markets, living rooms, and schools until it reached the newsrooms. All this commotion took her by surprise but with the help of Patty -her advice and support- she gathered enough courage to actually consider it. Soon came the interviews and polls. Not only the majority of people saw her as a smart and competent woman but as a strong and admirable widow of the man who could've change the country but fell victim of evil governments. As the talks of the people about Anais Echevarria being the first woman President got louder and louder, the national mourning of Vladimir Guzman faded more each hour: his assassination had become a national disillusion whereas the prospect of Mrs. Echevarria's presidential election represented the renewed national hope.

Behind all this was Patty. She, at the turn of the events, had morph from being her daughter into her mother's exclusive political advisor. Suddenly she'd gathered a team of 'International and Local Advisors' to speak *for* but never *to* her. The group, known as *Los Invisibles* by the mainstream media became her private army against the already-brewing attacks of the contenders as well as the brain of the campaign strategy and structure. Everything was happening too fast and too soon for her, thus Patty readily became her conscience as well as her subconscience. And with the slogan "For The Dawn of the New Way" the official Presidential race kicked off, now there was no turning back.

Discussions, interviews, meetings, speeches, visits, they all came and went and in the end what had to happen, did happened. She was elected the first woman President in the history of Peru, and if that wasn't enough, she made it in the first round gathering sixty percent of the votes. Now came the laughs, the tears, the screams, the hugs, the congratulatory calls and the inevitable blossoming of new enemies.

'Congratulations Mrs. President'. Said Patty to her mother, both clinking their champagne glasses in the private room. 'So, what will be your first actions Mrs. President?'

'Oh, stop calling me that Patricia'.

'Why? you better get used to it, for you are not only the President, but the first woman President, don't you see, you're making history!' They toasted again and neither of them could wipe the smile off their faces.

'Yes, we're making history darling, and your father would be so proud'.

'Well, you better watch it, because now they might wanna find you a First Man'. Both let off a series of laughter.

Order Out of Chaos

'You mean First Gentleman'. Anais said between coughs of laughter.

'Whatever you call it'.

'So that makes you the First Daughter'.

'I've always been the first and only daughter'.

'Yes you have. Yes you have'.

Patricia Echevarria, at twentynine, would turn out to be the most powerful woman in her country. Although she held no official position, she headed the advisory team with ten other members, all suggested by her, and appointed by her mother, the President. The restructuralization of the governmental body had been achieved firm and swiftly. The country was now being flooded by offers from the largest transnationals to invest millions in the many industries that had been neglected for so long. International Organizations, like the World Bank, suddenly approved loans that had been previously denied, repeatedly over the years. Anais Echevarria accepted an exclusive interview with one of America's biggest selling magazines, to later become its 'Person of the Year'. That same year Patricia Echevarria had moved from the salons of the Presidential Palace, to the smaller offices of the National Intelligence Service, and the body of Romulo Guzman a.k.a. Rocoto Relleno had been found washed up in the banks of the river

Gino Gianoli

Rimac, miles away from Lima, in such a decomposed stage that could only be identified by his teeth.

Baden Baden, Germany

'Many years ago,' Related Aesma Daeva to Vladimir Guzman as they walked through the forest. 'around these places, there were people who lived in peace and harmony with a well structured society who worshiped the moon and her mysteries'. Vladimir Guzman was spending some time away from France where he'd just been granted political asylum; and responding to the invitation from his dear friend and mentor, he'd arrived to this city of hot mineral springs in the early days of autumn. Alone, the two of them walked through the forest, thick in wood and acid rain, in sweaters, long pants and boots; one speaking revelation, the other about to be baptized in ancient insight.

'They carried a certain sacred knowledge from their ancestors who thousands of years before them, had developed their own civilization, while the rest of humanity were still hunter-gatherers. These people and their advance society suddenly vanished. Some believed a natural catastrophe as the cause, others, that it was their own knowledge that destroyed them. However, some of them survived and were scattered throughout the planet, where they started to build their own cities and societies with the help from the other underdeveloped homosapiens'.

'The people that lived here hundreds of years ago, believed that they were direct descendants of those first illuminated ones, whom some called the Vril People, others, the Shining Ones, and although they were aware that after the Great Catastrophe they scattered to different parts of the Earth, the leaders and their immediate family ended up in this part of Europe, in these forests. They believed that even though all civilizations on this planet were developed by different people under Vril influence, they were -after several generations later- all absorbed by the lower species of homosapiens: their knowledge, standards, beliefs, customs and raze were infested, sort-of-speak, by these species. Only the ones who resided in these lands are believed to have maintained their lineage pure; these people were known as The Ancestors. Their knowledge kept expanding as well as their people, whereas the other civilizations ceased to advance in such pace. It was at this stage where The Ancestors evolved from astrologers into astronomers, from alchemists into chemists; they went from priesthood to science and from mystery to knowledge'.

'These people undoubtedly had to had some interbreeding with the lower species, for it meant the survival and spread of their knowledge, but as opposed to the other civilizations, *they* absorbed the lower species, not the other way around. Thousands of years had past since their people taught and built such early civilizations as the Sumerian, Persian, Egyptian, and sailed off to other continents. Then the direct descendants of the Shining Ones built Athens and gave the world the gift of philosophy. Other branches of the First People, who by now were recognized in its inner-circles as the Vril Society, years later created Rome and supported its ever expanding empire, for they realized that in order for them and their knowledge to survive they must spread. The Society's objectives by this stage had long shifted from purely cultural to a more ambitious and politically active purpose: To unite the world for the improvement of mankind and his survival, thus The Order was born'.

'But we know, my dear friend Vladimir, how corrupted and weak the Empire turned when its leaders lost sight of the original objective, leading it to its unavoidable demise and take-over; but those were the catastrophic results of innerbreeding: they wanted the future emperors to be pure blooded and what they got were demented quasi-gods in love with themselves. All the while people worshiped their own gods who in reality represented nature itself, but overall the true god was knowledge of the world. But then something very wrong happened'.

'Out of the east not only came hordes of underdeveloped people set on taking over the west by force, but also spread a notion of a one god, the God, that took the form of a fatherly figure who demanded complete attention and adoration and tolerated any other god, imposing fear and guilt in the heart of men. This God claimed the weak as its chosen ones: the slaves and the impaired, the sick and underdeveloped. The people of the world were aghast at first but later dismissed those ideas as delusional, irrelevant yet understandable: the slaves needed a god, a hope. Mankind seemed busy developing, inventing, discovering; technology was definitely gathering speed, but no one suspected that this notion, of a one-God, was gathering as much speed and as many believers as well'.

'So it was that at the first sign of alarm one of the Emperors decided to persecute the one-God followers that were calling themselves Christians, named after the revolutionary jewish carpenter named Jesus who these people thought was the Christ, throughout the Empire only making them seem the more glorious and pious as they'd die for their one-God. This Emperor, our dear Tiberius that is, made martyrs out of these lunatics, so instead of radicalizing the problem, he singlehandedly turned it into a meaningful movement and powerful cause'.

'And just to say something about this character Jesus, my dear friend Vladimir, he was, as I said before, a revolutionary. Yes, yes indeed, he rebelled against the Empire and formed his army, an army that carried no weapons but something more lethal: ideas. That is what was great about this Jesus character. But did you know where he got these ideas from? I'll tell you'.

'In Egypt there was a clan. This Clan were illuminated people descendants from the Shining Ones that had somehow maintained the bloodline unpolluted; they considered themselves the last pure representatives of the Vril People and were complete hermits who lived in caves in the desert and studied the old scriptures past on by their forefathers. At the same time they would write what they learned and their discoveries. They were meditators and foreseers as well. A young man of approximately fifteen years of age, according to the Clan's ancient scriptures, was taken to visit the Clan by his father to hopefully become one of them, only to be promptly rejected on the basis that he was not a descendant of the illuminated ones. Now, even though the young boy wasn't a descendant of the first People he was indeed special. He, again, according to the Clan's scriptures, seemed eager to learn and to rebel against the world, his world. In the years he spent with the Clansmen he was told about the one-God notion, and how this god had convinced first the Sumerians and their descendants the Assyrians and since the Jews were their slaves, they were converted as well. But these people were weak and had many innerconflicts, the Assyrians had ceased to exist, so it was up to the Jewish people to carry the torch, but they either were expelled out of any land they occupied, or became slaves -the Egyptians, for instance, held them as slaves for seven hundred years. The one-God, whom the Jews called Yahweh, needed something new, a new face, and fast or it ran the risk of irrelevance'.

'When the rebellious young boy heard this, and meditated and pondered and wondered, he realized that his time had come: He was going to carry the torch, he was willing to be this new face, this new breath of fresh air for Yahweh the god of his people. He saw himself as the Liberator of the Jewish people from the Romans -which was his main objective- and the savior of their faith. And thus, years later, the young foreigner went back to his homeland to speak of new ideas about old Yahweh'.

'Although the Clan's scriptures never stipulate the young man's name, it does clearly recount what this young man told them after he came back to the Clansmen caves running from authorities and in search for shelter. He had spoken the New Word: Yahweh wasn't only demanding but he was compassionate too, He wanted to award everyone with eternal life in Heaven if they did what he ordered. But to the young man Yahweh was the mask and impulse for his hidden agenda, his real motivation to change the world: revolution against the Romans. Also, what he didn't counted on was the hostility from his own jewish comrades, especially the rabbis whom had had enough when he called himself the Son of God. He had also learned from the Clansmen about the eventual fall of the great Empire and the impossibility of a reign by Yahweh the one-God, since what this god essentially demanded was faith instead of knowledge and that completely contradicted the human approach to the world; what this god asked was blind obedience of his laws and acceptance of his infallible nature. This insight was taken by the young man as a hidden clue as to how to maintain and spread the word of Yahweh who would later became known as Allah. He also was smart enough to warn his people of the coming of the Antichrist, the one who would lie, seduce and enslave mankind at the end of days, in order to prepare them for the eventual decay of Yahweh's reign. But things got too hot and complicated for the young man, who by now there's no denying was Jesus, and soon he became an outlaw, wanted by both the Roman authorities and Jewish Clerics. What happened to him at the end is very unclear. Many people believe he died in that cross, however, the Clansmen scriptures contain this account and goes even further to state that the young foreigner managed to avoid detention and lived near by, married, had kids and died of old age full of remorse and guilt at hearing about the hundreds of thousands of people that died for the failed revolution and association with him'.

'Little did he know that the renewed and improved Jewish faith, now called Christianity, would conquer the Empire, due to political reasons, and thus the western world, bringing the Society's objective to a complete halt for hundreds of years. The Order, became object of persecution for its paganism and conquered by the notion of Christianity. Now everyone had to worship the one-God Yahweh and his son as well. In the east, Yahweh changed his name to Allah and found another revolutionary, an illiterate yet successful business man named Muhammed, to lead his warriors out of the Arabic peninsula and into the east and west. Now there was no place in the world where this people, The Illuminated Ones, could worship their gods or expand their knowledge; actually, knowledge itself became the enemy: the Dark Ages came over us'.

'The Dark Ages signified the lowest point in the existence of the descendants of the Vril Society, and therefore mankind itself, and the highest stage in the reign of Yahweh the one-God. The few remaining groups of Illuminated people had been gathering in secret since the time of the Christian take-over of the Empire to worship their gods and to keep knowledge alive and striving since they knew that this was the only weapon they had, and only hope they harbored, against the mass-numbing of the people under the one-God rule, who by then had appointed a human representative called the Pope, who had more power than any King of the day, to rule and influence the many tiny and scattered kingdoms in all of Europe. One way that The Illuminated Ones managed not only to stay alive but to actually make any changes, was to infiltrate the army and the King's Courts. During this time the followers of Yahweh and Allah took radical positions and perceived the other as infidel, not knowing, or in fact forgetting, their one source. The Pope, demanded that the holy land, Jerusalem, be rid of those heretics, that called themselves Moslems at any cost and so the Crusades began. The Illuminated Ones saw this as a chance to infiltrate knowledge to people who had been secluded from foreign influence for hundreds of years. The legions of knights who rode east were made up mostly by Illuminated Ones who've established connections with their eastern alikes. And it was them, The

Illuminated Ones who influenced the Pope and Kings to continue the Crusades for hundreds of years, thus allowing trade to flourish once again'.

'First it was trade then art which took the western world out of its dark confines. The Rennaisance meant the first liberation of the human mind by Illuminated artists; until then, God and his son had taken the central role or main character in painting and sculpture as well as then-modern architecture was solely utilized and implemented in the construction of massive cathedrals and domes. After the Rennaisance, Man himself took the main role in art: the first step toward global illumination. Then came the Enlightment and the first attempt at the liberalization of the mind. The fall of all Monarchies became imminent and necessary. Although the Church was still very influential in government matters, it had significantly lost its previous powers. But just as the Church was receding its grip and influence, the Monarchies became stronger and crueler. The world needed revolution. The Illuminated Ones weren't persecuted any longer and had grown in members. Now it was not necessary to be a descendant of the Vril Society to join but one had to be a scholar of some kind, or in the least, occupy a high office in the government or kingdom. By this time, another chapter of the Illuminated Ones were already fighting the British Crown in

America, which they would defeat a short time later. They, the American Illuminated, would pressure its European brothers to begin the revolution at home. That would eventually lead to the French Revolution and the beginning of the end of the Monarchies'.

'One can only imagine how they rejoiced after the fall of the French Monarchy, how far they had come, and how much more it needed to be done. After establishing themselves in powerful circles in France and the British Isles, then came the unification of Germany and Italy, when those countries were just a bunch of messy statelets in the heart of Europe, and the infiltration in the remaining Monarchies. But since the road isn't always smooth, one must make it smooth if one is to get to his destination, that is why, my dear Vladimir, the Order as we call it, has never been shy of getting rid of whomever got in the way, it has been done from the beginning and it is done so now, as you well know. Some other times it had been done to start something'.

'Our first try at the unification of countries began with the assassination of Archduke Ferninand of Austria. That triggered the first big war, after which, we suggested the creation of the "League of Nations" which we both know failed. So some years later we had a second go after World War II, this time we were much successful and the result was the

United Nations. Now, you must understand, that in a world where Man have been shackled and blindfolded for so long by religion, we must have had to act with the utmost discretion and secrecy, all for the sole purpose of exposing the truth and spread the knowledge, the only thing that will set Man free'.

'We admit there were some catastrophic results in several of our experiments to unite the world, but the end shall justify the means. For instance in order for the notion of a entity such as the United Nations to exist there had to be a reason. The reason was the Soviet Union. We, my friend, helped Lenin and his Bolsheviks take over Czarist Russia. Do you really think such a minuscule and incompetent group of young hungry revolutionaries could've taken ahold of power as fast and as violent as they did, all by themselves? I don't think so my friend, but we needed an enemy and he provided the perfect one: Communism. All the killing that took place after he took power, that worsened with Stalin, was something no one had counted on. The same should be said about our friend Hitler who, according to records, just lost it; lost his mind in power; the same back-firing effect happened to us years before with Napoleon: They somehow lost their mind on their way to our objective, and that is because their minds weren't trained enough to managed such vast power.

I can assure you now, my friend, we've gotten better, much, much better. Trial and error is the key. Just take a look at our new monarchs: our CEO's and Presidents, with a few exceptions I can tell you that the objectives are being met by our brethren, not only for The Order, but for Mankind'.

'So, now my friend, we have united Europe, next will be Asia and the Americas, then the rest of the world; and you will be there to celebrate with us as we'll rejoice in seeing such day dawn on us, the day of the end of the endless struggle of our forefathers: to bring order out of chaos. For it is control, my dear Vladimir, that which brings the greatest freedom'.

Vladimir remained in silence as they stepped out of the woods. He knew that by being given this revelation he was tacitly considered one of them in the high ranks of The Order. He wanted to ask him if indeed he was, or maybe, if he himself was a descendant of those people he was talking about, but he didn't dare ask. He figured if he was, then he will find out. The black Mercedez stood waiting, with the chauffeur standing by its side.

Aesma Daeva lead him to a path that took them to a cottage on top of a hill, covered in green. Inside they took their long coats off and sat by the fire place sipping on cognac. They remained in silence staring at the flames dancing and vanishing, and reappearing again, giving off their cracking whispers.

'It all comes down to good versus evil doesn't it?' Aesma Daeva uttered to the flames. 'Two thousand years have past since they effectively took over the world, they had their chance, they've prepared their people…for they knew this moment will come'.

'Our moment…' Vladimir said tentatively. Aesma Daeva remained in silence.

And so she waited. Hours passed by before anyone would give her any information about the missing patient.

'Ohhh yeahh...' Said the receptionist. 'You're here 'bout the crazy guy who walked outta here right, last week?' Lara bit her lip.

'Yes...m'am, I've been here for almost two hours waiting for someone to come to talk to me'.

'Mmmhmm'. Replied the jumbo receptionist, nonchalant, not a worry in her forehead; her long and curved purple nails with sparkles and stripes, flipped the pages of her magazine. 'Well, the docta in charge, won't be here till six o'clock'. It was four, and she had been there since two.

'Why couldn't you tell me that two hours ago when I asked you about this matter?' Lara knew that question was as futile as asking her for help, eventhough that was her job. She thought about shooting her instead, in her big fat round lazy face. 'Can you give me the Doctor's name please?'

With a great struggle, the colossal representation of a woman, rolled her chair to the side and pulled yet another file, again, the long curved nails did the flipping; it seemed as if she was taking her sweet ass time, as if she was actually enjoying this. Lara had shot her six times in her mind. The phone rang and she picked it up. Now this was going to take even longer.

Lara walked out of the hospital and headed to the beach, she was exhausted. Fortunately the sun was sinking far behind her and the few people that were still there, began to vacate the sands. Wearing nothing but her panties, Lara ran into the coming waves, swam, and let her body float and wobble in the warm blue waters of Miami Beach while she stared at the cloudless sky, infinitely.

Back on the sand she realized that it was Saturday and immediately thought about the 'Bridge Crawlers', Where were they? Was it Saturday or Sunday that they crawled in and crowded the beaches? In the past, under no circumstances, would she ever dared to come to the beach on a Saturday or Sunday.

Every once in a while a slightly cool breeze would whiff by awaking her pink nipples and skin hairs. Her body dried and roasted slowly as she laid there on the bare sand; her memories and plans mingled and danced, her breathing regulated and her heart lounged; she was completely relaxed and serene until a young girl passing out flyers suddenly appeared and handed her a pamphlet of some kind, telling her about time running out and some new word. Of course she took the pamphlet but it remained in her hands as she laid back, half sleep, hypnotized by the soothing sound of the crashing waves in the background and enveloped by the fresh seabreeze which would've taken the pamphlet to fly away if it wasn't stuck, flapping, in between her fingers. And with the vivid memory of Patty and the shower scene, her kisses and caresses, she descended into the arms of Morpheus; she dreamed of Eddie and how he was upset at her for making him abandon his mother to run away with her; she dreamed of her mother, Betty, and her father who didn't have a face; and finally she dreamed about Timothy and the suitcase: she saw how he exchanged the packets of merchandise for the ones with baby powder. Then she saw him at the beach with her, he seemed younger and wiser; he whispered something to her ear and that's when she awoke.

After shaking her sleep off, she took a look at the pink flyer in her hand.

Time is Running Out
The New Word is Here
The Celebration has Began

Inside it explained in concise detail the meaning of the New Word and the signs of the coming of The Prophet, who shall revitalize the word of God. This Prophet had already been found and was preparing his people to start their revolution in the hearts of men, and in what better place than Miami Beach where everyone is so corrupted by false beauty and money. Then the pamphlet went on to indicate where anyone interested in being part of the imminent change could join or inquire about this group of mystic revolutionaries.

Lara meditated on this for a long time as if she had found a clue that didn't want to reveal more. It had gotten really dark and turned a little chilly, she put her clothes back on and took a look around: she wasn't the only one at the beach, there were still a few people there. Her watch marked 11:20 pm. Was it that late? The sound of music from the streets signaled the beginning of the nightlife.

She gathered her stuff and headed off the sand towards the restaurant with the flyer in her hand.

Behind her, in the distant horizon, heavy clouds began to gather.

After the chants, everyone retired out of the living room, making it look larger and emptier. Only Timothy and the young man, Babeuf, stayed sitting on the floor. Babeuf inquired about Timothy's wounds and hunger and then told him about that night in the alley with the three derelicts; two days had passed since.

'You happened to be there right on time my friend'. Timothy told him.

'I doubt it was mere coincidence'. Babeuf responded.

'What do you mean?'

'I mean that I knew you were going to be there, and I was supposed to save you'.

'I'm sorry but…What do you mean?'

'Don't you realize? Hasn't the truth been revealed to you yet?'

Timothy didn't quite know what to say, he wasn't sure whether to admit to this strange fellow he'd been hearing voices, for the past week, eversince he awoke -much in the same way he awoke here: beaten and wounded- at some beach, last Sunday. And he was just about to say it but Babeuf started first.

'Allow me to share my revelation with you'. He stared at Timothy as if waiting for him to do, or say something; his eyes, green, seemed excited and lost, his black and greasy hairs fell over his unshaven cheeks down his shoulders like pitch-black cascades and his trembling hands reached to his shirt pocket in search for a cigarette.

'I will be as direct as possible with you, for we're running out of time'. He then proceeded to nervously light the cigarette, while Timothy just sat looking at him, transfixed. 'This, revelation…was first revealed to me at the age of sixteen, my parents of course thought I was insane, I did too for a while until the voices became visions'. His speech, pronunciation and delivery indicated some kind of education and well up-bringing. 'I was shown, in conscious dreams, the imminent changes that would take place in the world as we know it. The voices and the visions were clear in their message: prepare the people of God for the tribulation is upon us.'

'I know what you're thinking, you've heard this many, many times before: people announcing the end of the world, lunatics yelling armageddon's here, doomsday junkies pointing at the signs of the end of time; I, too have heard and chose to ignored such blah, blah, blah; but what I'm about to tell you is something you already know but don't know what it is, something you've been searching for since you became conscious for the first time'. Timothy began to sweat cold underneath his dirty shirt and ragged pants, he felt light and dizzy as if he was about to faint.

'For a long, long time the voices and visions have announced the coming of the New Prophet to renew The Word. For thousands of years there have been attempts to get rid of us and the way of Yahweh, the one-God, but we have time and again come out victorious of these battles of the mind and soul, and the only reason we've been so successful is because we've diversified, we've adapted to the region and mentality and molded The Word to its environment and time. Thus we managed to spread throughout the planet with different names and colors and practices but maintaining the same core: love and fear of the one-God, the God of the meek'. The light smoke coming out of his mouth and nostrils took the shape of snakes floating upwards just enough to hover above their heads.

'But now history find us at our weakest,' Babeuf continued. 'they're about to take over and they know that; unless, someone gives us a new breath of fresh air just like the old prophets did in their time. And so a couple of days ago, it was revealed to me in a dream, that I would finally find this New Prophet, he will come out of the oceans torned and beaten, hungry and weak; and I would provide him with shelter and food and revelation: something his heart already knows, and we shall have a New Word and a leader and a chance at survival for another millennia, at least.

'So now I tell you, my friend; you are the One; the One they fear; the Prophet, our Savior'.

Timothy, although astonished, to say the least, felt reassurance and strength rushing forth from within and suddenly the voices that tormented him, sounded clear and beautiful, a musical harmony, pure immanence. But he still had one last skeptic worm slithering in his head:

'How do you know it's me, this New Prophet you're looking for?'

Babeuf drew a satisfied smile and took a long last drag.

'The voices were clear about the day but not the time or place where I'd find you, so I wondered the streets for a while relying on the only clear clues I had: your signs'.

'My signs, what signs?'

Babeuf raised his gaze from his eyes to his forehead. 'In your forehead, that's the sign of the third eye'.

Timothy slowly proceeded to touch it and rub it, softly. After a moment of reflection he asked: 'What's the other?'

He, again, raised his gaze a little higher still. 'Your hair. The color of your hair is the color of the one who was reborn, the one who escaped his first destiny'.

Now, he had no doubt.

Is denial really that harmful? If one doesn't suppress the traumas that afflict the soul how would one get on with life? How would Lara have a clear mind to find and dispose of her new Target? In her world, denial was as essential as her weapon and she used it as such.

By the time she arrived the restaurant was closed, Serge and the rest of the staff where finishing putting the chairs upsidedown on the tables and cleaning their stations. She knocked on the glass door and asked for Francis when one of the busboys answered. Francis sat in the crowded tiny office running the day's report and making next week schedule when Lara appeared.

'Oh hi detective…'

'Rommel,' Answered Lara. 'please call me Alicia'.

'Right, what can I do for you Alicia'. Francis noticed her appearance: tanned face, unwashed hair, skirt and blouse wrinkled and with sand. 'Are you okay?'

'Oh yeah, I'm okay, just came from the beach'.

'I see that'. The old office clock marked 12:00 am.

'I came to tell you that I have a pretty good idea where Timothy might be'. Francis's eyes widened and her mouth opened slightly.

'Where?'

'First I'd have to take a shower, let's go to your place'. Francis dropped the daily report and schedule, grabbed her keys, locked the office door, ordered everyone to stop doing whatever they where doing and go home.

'Okay, let's go.' She said to Lara turning all the lights off.

And so when Timothy Moone finally and fully realized and accepted his fate, his new fate that is, there was no room for denial in his heart or in his mind; the voices themselves had evicted any sign of such from his new self.

The old house where he and the community lived, was located in the poor side of town, the house itself was deteriorating with its front and back yards grassless and dry as a bone. Curiously, none of the rooms seemed to have doors, in fact, the only door was found in the main entrance. Living and dining rooms were semi empty; rugs and cushions, dirty and ripping at the seams, were the only objects found there. Everyone ate at the same time, around noon, their one and only meal for the day, and when they gathered to eat no one spoke a word, not even the children. The residents of the old house came and went as they pleased, mostly the men and young women ventured outside to distribute flyers and invitations to their once a month gatherings held in the patio and backyard, the older women stayed in the old house, some cooked, others cared after the children. There was no doubt that Babeuf was their spiritual leader and CFO.

Timothy stepped inside the rusted and stained bathtub next to his room, filled with warm water which was carried in buckets from the main faucet downstairs by two young women. There he tried to rest, to cleanse his body and wash his scattered wounds but even the bathroom didn't have a door, and this made him feel as if he was being watched. Once again tiredness proved heavier than uncomfort. So he fell asleep as soon as he stepped out of the tub. Lying on the feeble and ripped mattress on the floor, he dreamed of the future; the next day; the day of revelation.

Gino Gianoli

Miami Beach, U.S.

    Miami certainly appears so much more colorful and brighter and cleaner when coming from Lima. It's its distinct air, its different smell, its certain newness; like a child born into a rich and powerful family. That is how he saw Miami on his way back. He dropped his luggage at the door and himself on the couch; then, attempted to call the restaurant and let Francis know he was back but exhaustion made his body heavy and tiredness pulled his eyelids shut; memories were dancing with dreams and in his mind he did managed to pick up the phone and dial…and talk to her…yeah, but that was the beginning of his dream…

    Minutes later, or maybe hours later, he found himself in the restaurant. Wait a second, maybe it had been days later, that he realized himself sitting in table twelve with Francis. He knew exactly why they were there. Serge the busboy had been promoted to server and was trying to uncork the bottle of wine. Francis, she looked gorgeous and excited like a child. The restaurant it self seemed different somehow, a bit more spacious and newer. As the wine was being poured he saw he was wearing a tuxedo and she wouldn't look anywhere else but his face. As Serge retired she lifted her glass and he did the same. 'To good fortune and fruitful days to come'. She smile that satisfied smile, the glasses clinked, and they let the bloody red fluid invade their mouths. Timothy knew what she was going to say next.

'Timothy,' Her voice gathering courage. 'you know we've been…um…together, for quite some time now…' And she was saying it. Or at least trying to say it, but finding the way there was more difficult than imagined, so she took several linguistic detours and soon found herself in a syntaxic labyrinth that urged her to take another sip of wine with hopes to lubricate that stuttering tongue of hers. 'What I'm trying to say is…' And once again she tried as he knew the inevitable question was going to be asked eventually, as soon as she'd find the words.

That pseudo-relationship began like so many others: by accident. Francis took the job as manager of Timothy Moone's restaurant as soon as he opened it. They met through an acquaintance and she seemed perfect for the position: strong, hard-worker, sexy, loyal, and with great people skills. She had become the heart and soul of the restaurant while Timothy Moone's presence was intermittent, but he always made sure to be on top of every little detail or problem or change in the establishment;

even to meet personally, the new hires as soon as possible.

What once crossed his mind and was quickly dismissed became reality: she being interested in him. But he had always esteemed her as an intelligent woman that knew better than to fall for her boss, because it could cost her her job and him the headache of finding someone else like her for the position, which was unlikely. But logic is not an easy word to find in the dictionary of lust. It all began as it always begins; first, their looks at each other lasted a bit longer than necessary; then, their tone of voice became sweeter; and laughs originated from anything and more frequently than before. So, the first-inevitable had to happen: One saturday after a busy night, they stayed, after everyone had gone, for a couple of drinks as the shift and sale reports were running. Their kiss was urgent and reluctant, it had the taste of newness, freshness, fire and danger. They both knew this couldn't possibly turn out good, but there they were, lips locked and tongues bound. It was too late to turn back, they had made a pact with the devil, they've turned careers for lust, professionalism for heat, logic for hormones. And they knew it. Even in the middle of biting and grabbing and pulling and sucking, she asked him: 'What's gonna happen?' But even that question instead of bringing reason to their heads it caused more arousal in their naked bodies since it represented forbiddance.

The game -for they agreed to keep it a secret game- continue and intensified. Now they met three times a week instead of once. Their time together expanded from her bed to movies and restaurants and walks. Gifts began to be exchanged and unimportant 'work-related' calls started -all mostly from her part- and all the while implicitly emphasizing the no-strings-attached policy.

So the second-inevitable had to happen: someone had to fall in love. Someone always does. And that is why they're sitting there, one trying to untie her tongue, the other filling his glass for the fourth time.

Finally he decided to end this tongue twister and say what she wanted to.

'Francis, stop please, stop. What you wanna know is where we stand, correct?' Her expression revealed as if some kind of weigh was lifted off her shoulders -or shall we say, tongue- and at the same time it showed a certain fear of what the answer might be. 'Well, to tell you the truth,' Answering to his own question he thought of each word as he pronounced them. 'I don't think it would be a good idea for us to continue,' His pause was due to the sudden slight contortion of her eyes, as if she had been poked in her chest, and silent inhales.

'…To…continue this, whatever this is, I…really like you and everything but…I don't think…' Her eyes filled, and her jaws clenched as her breathing became audible. 'Please, Francis, damn it! we knew this was…'

With the last bits of self control vanishing, she managed to let out:

'A game?! just a game!' She said before her voiced cracked, as the dam in her heart began crumbling down. And now, Timothy thought, the third-inevitable will happen: She will either leave the restaurant or we just won't be able to work together. And as she sat with her head bent down, crying on her glass of wine; and him, right across staring at her with a pained expression on his face and his blue hair undone; Serge approached him and whispered in his ear:

'Sir, there're some gentlemen outside waiting for you'. Timothy turned to face Serge but instead found Vladimir Guzman, with a bullet hole in his forehead, bending over his shoulders holding a knife in his right hand and with the left pulling his head back exposing his throat which was quickly slit. As he fell to the floor, flooded in blood and feeling coldness spreading rapidly from his feet to his torso, he saw Francis stand over him, glass of wine in her hand, with the worst expression of contempt he'd ever seen; she kneeled and whispered venomously: 'Tomorrow you'll begin dying'.

He didn't know where he was; whether his eyes were open or shut; his living room was in complete darkness and numbing silence. The airconditioner had dropped the temperature to 50 degrees and he found himself freezing. After turning on the lights and A/C off, he picked up the phone and dialed the restaurant. He rubbed his neck with a certain morbid feeling of satisfaction: a feeling of appreciation for things we take for granted and the satisfaction of knowing it is still there after the thought of it being gone. Ten rings later he realized it must be closed. The kitchen clock marked 2:30 am and he wondered how long did he sleep, while he walked, naked, to the patio; slid the glassdoors wide open to let the breeze in, stepped out and stopped at the edge of the pool. The night was perfect: light breeze, quiet, pure air, half moon…all he needed was to jump in and refresh his body, then, he remembered.

In three jumps he was back where he had dropped his luggage, on his knees, rummaging through clothes and papers. Finally he fished out a piece of paper; actually a paper napkin. A number scribbled; a phone number; Lara Walker's phone number.

Without thinking, he dialed and waited. It was ringing. On the fourth one she answered.

Is there such a thing as love at first sight? I guess it all depends on the outcome: if the people involved end up together, better yet, married, then everyone will agree that it was certainly love. But if they don't, then it will be dismissed as just a temporary obsession for someone; infatuation, fascination, fixation etc.

Everything and everyone are judge by their outcome.

The next day they met for lunch in a quaint little Bistro on *Española Way* hiding from the dirty commotion of Washington Avenue and its car and people traffic. They chose a table in the shade and ordered bloodymarys. To Lara Walker, he looked as interesting as a new word; to Timothy Moone, she appeared as perfect as that morning: warm and embracing, sunny and brightly hopeful. Their conversation began with a cautious pace, and it spanned from art to fashion, from food to sex, always bouncing from theme to theme but never landing on the subject of their employment or employers.

Although they had met each other almost a week ago, they hadn't had a chance to really talk about anything but business. The first time being in that churrasqueria in Lima seemed so long ago. After that they met in a house where they were given last details of their Target. There they only looked and thought about each other as partners. That evening Patricia Echevarria introduced them to Rocoto Relleno who had everything detailed in print: Where the target was going to stand that night, the amount of people around him, even an approximate number of the people who would show up for the outdoor speech; he'd also had arranged the houses on the hill where they would set up shop, entering and exit routes, vehicles, etcetera.

'How do you know he would be standing here exactly?' Asked Timothy pointing at the diagram. Lara was about to translate this to Rocoto Relleno in spanish. But he drew a smile that made the tiny craters on his cheeks enlarge, and answered himself instead .

'Becoz I know heem as if hee waz my zon'.

Timothy knew exactly why Vladimir Guzman had become a target. The only thing that was still pinching his brain was if they knew about his relationship with him. If they knew I would've been dead already, he thought.

The next morning passed by uneventful, waiting for the call, which came at around five o' clock. A white van waited for him downstairs and took him for a ride across the city. Sitting there looking out the window he saw how as they got further and further from his hotel, the landscape became more arid and dirtier, more poor and abandoned.

Gino Gianoli

Kilometers later the van climbed up a dirt road sided by huts made with straw material and others with adobe. He tried to ask how far more to go, to the driver, but this one replied something about no speekee; so he remained quiet. It had gotten dark and since there were no street posts, the headlights were the only source of light. Suddenly the van halted in its tracks. It seemed like the middle of nowhere.

'Out!' yelled the driver. He stepped out to find hordes of people running by, it seemed like if there was a big fire they were running from. Everyone seemed to be heading down the dirt road, excited and hurried. He took one last look at the driver and he pointed to a hut. 'Der yu go in'. And he took off leaving a dark cloud of dirt and diesel.

The hut didn't seem like much, the automatic rifle was in place and next to it a radio, but the view was perfect: 180 degrees panorama at the plaza below and its surroundings, right across, some kind of a huge balcony had being set up with banners and spotlights on its sides. What else can I ask for? he thought. Down below hundreds of people were gathering and dancing to the rhythms from the orchestra playing very loud by the side of the balcony. Timothy Moone stared down at the crowd, lost in thought; then came a noise, followed by a voice on the radio.

'Yes?' He answered.

'Hello there'. Lara Walker's voice sounded distorted but recognizable.

'Where are you pretty lady?' He walked to the window, that was actually a hole.

'All the way on the other side, and I'm looking at you through the telescope in my rifle'. He had to smile.

'Really? and what do you see?' He walked away from the window.

'Nothing now, but I bet you're still smiling'.

As the crowd-warmer screamed through the speakers chants and slogans, he was seen through the lenses of both rifles as they prepared for the real thing. Then the crowd got louder and a roar expanded in the air, like in a concert when the lights go down and the band walks on stage. Lara Walker's voice came on again.

'Ready?' He replied the same as a confirmation, and added:

'See you in Miami'.

Through his lens Timothy Moone saw the same man that in one way or the other had believed in him and made him so much money. It was because of Vladimir Guzman that the organization took him in; he'd been the one that recommended him to Baphomet.

Meanwhile in Lara's post, she was lying in aiming position, looking through the lens and shaking her head in disapproval of the 2001 space odyssey soundtrack being played, as he walked on stage. 'How tacky!' She said while Timothy, aiming his weapon, felt admiration and pity for the man at the end of the lens.

'He looks so grand, so...' He said to himself.

People were chanting his name with their hearts. They really love this man, he thought. The voice on the radio came on again.

'Twenty seconds'. He adjusted his focus and countercounted.

Nineteen...eighteen...seventeen...

The roar had increased dramatically, it seemed as if it came from right outside the hut. His vision was clear when he saw Vladimir Guzman take a hit, while he was still counting. He lifted his head up in the direction of Lara, then return to his lens. He saw the second shot and how Vladimir stepped back, he adjusted his focus and shot. His bullet had barely missed Vladimir's forehead and landed on the person next to him, literally blowing her face up. He let off a quick exhale and took a deep one in. He aimed at the moving Target and shot. The voice on the radio announced that the Target was down, repeat, the Target's down. Only days later he would

Order Out of Chaos

find out that his second shot ripped through Vladimir's neck.

And four days later, sitting across from each other in this sunny and simple day, with their bloodymarys halfway done, they knew that there was something special about the other, something they had either never seen or hadn't seen in a long, long time. So when their cautious and superfluous conversations worn thin and there was nothing left to say or deny; it was their eyes that held each other in a trembling stare, each relying on the other not to look away, both shutting their ears off and hands crawling on the table imperceptibly; fingertips in search of fingertips; pheromones firing away with everything they had; necks steadily stretching and lips slowly parting; saliva rushing and tongues awaiting.

No one remembers how they got to the penthouse. Next thing Lara remembers, if we were to ask her, is being thrown on the rug in the living room; her belly being kissed and sucked by Timothy while her pants were taken off slowly. How many times did the tip of his nose rubbed against her craving lips behind the thin veil of the panties as he kissed her inner thighs? She dipped in ecstasy and lost herself willingly in the fluid eruption of her desire, while she stared at the blueness of the sky through the glass doors of the terrace. It was the penthouse at the Lowes where Lara Walker had checked in under another name. She loved the view from the terrace and it was there where they found themselves next, tumbling, rolling, never letting go from the other, kissing every part of their bodies repeatedly with fury and hunger. Then, hours later, they submerged in the bathtub, so large it resembled a miniature pool. The warm water pretty soon turned into foam, 'peach scented bubbles' said Lara. They stared at each other's face which was the only part of the body visible. Under the bubbles their legs rubbed against one another and their hands wandered in every direction and into every orifice.

In the bedroom, still wet, they laid naked on the bed staring at the ceiling above, contented, perfectly happy, surrounded by whiteness all around the room and the blueness from the sky. Timothy cut several lines of coke on a mirror and proceeded to sniff a couple.

'Refuel'. He said and offered some. Lara was went ahead and did her share.

It felt good and right, the kind of moment that if it'd only last forever...one would never get tire. So if situations and people were judge by their outcomes, what was this then? Lust at first sight?

But it is in bed where confessions take place more often than in church. And on this white platform of feathers and silk, Timothy Moone said two things that would alter the course of his life. One: his intention to retire from the organization, since he had enough money and a legit business up and running; Two: he believed that he had found the one for him (Love at first sight?). The pained silence that followed this confession made him turn to her.

'What?'

'Listen, Timothy, I like you, I really do'.

'But?' He sat up.

'But, we've just met, not even a week ago, and you're talking about 'the one'? get ahold of yourself will you'. That was enough to stop him in his tracks, to stop him from railing off to looserville where he was definitely heading towards. He thought about it, staring at nothing, then drew a semi smile.

'You're right'. He said almost inaudible. 'I got a little carried away, and I apologize'.

Both remained relative quiet for a while, then he asked her for a favor. He needed to leave something with her. Before she could ask what was it, he had jumped out of the bed and into his clothes, picked up the phone and called for a cab.

'Don't you dare go anywhere, beautiful'. Blew her a kiss and out the door he went. Lara, still laying in bed, was left dumfounded and with the question in her mouth.

Downstairs, in the cab, he looked back as it was pulling off the ramp, to see this tall, white and trendy building in all its art-deco glory and minimalism. He looked at top where the penthouse was and thought: she was the one. And with all these thoughts rushing through his head and these feelings speeding and crashing and speeding again through his body; the notions of Francis and the restaurant remained irrelevant and forgotten.

New York City, U.S.

Sometimes we must do things ourselves if we want them to get done right. With this thought refusing to rest, he waited in front of the wall of glass in the large office looking out to the bustling city below. Unperturbed by the flowing cigar smoke that partly covered the view, he contemplated the bright light of day, the alive brick and metal structures reaching to the skies and the flowing streets below growing and transforming, in charge of the ever manipulation of nature. How far we've come since the days when we where lost in the snow not knowing north from south, in the jungles, in the forests. So there he stood, puffing, overlooking progress a la minute. The office where Baphomet waited was located on the twentyeighth floor of the United Nations building.

His slicked-back shiny hair, his tanned face, his slim figure and impeccable attire blended into a towering silhouette, as he stood in front of the glass wall with an explosion of early daylight behind him; turning around only when he heard the door opening. Enter Aesma Daeva. His expression of concern left no time for small talk. Sitting across each other, separated by the wide wooden desk, Baphomet took the guest's chair putting out his emblematic cigar; the other ordered through the intercom not to be bothered; now it was him whose physical features were somewhat diffused by the bright light coming in from behind.

'So, what's the situation?' The one behind the desk asked with a barely visible frown.

'It is very complex, and confusing, so I'll start from the beginning'. Responded Baphomet pulling out another cigar. 'Do you mind?' Aesma Daeva shook his head; clouds began to cover the sky behind him. After puffing it lit, he fished a file out of his leather suitcase, flipped through it and began:

'It seems that our friend, Timothy Moone, who has been working for us since '96 decided to go his own way,' Puff. 'obviously under the influence of our old pal Vladimir. They, plus one of our contacts in Egypt, a Frenchman named Bernard Bayard, formed a side project, as they called it, to infiltrate, negotiate, and sell our most valued product in that region of the world which, as you well know, is The Order's strategical region of distribution'. He puffed again.

'So, as we informed you, based on the evidence we gathered Vladimir Guzman unfortunately became a Prime Target, he had already been reelected President and we had to move fast'. He paused to re-lit his cigar. 'I myself arranged for Mr. Moone and Ms. Walker to be the ones to carry out this mission, for several reasons: one, because they're among the best we have; two, to observe how would Mr. Moone react to the fact that he had to take his leading accomplice out; and three, in the case that Mr. Moone would have a last minute guilt trip or felt that he had some kind of loyalty to him, I still had Ms. Walker whom could've taken out the Target all by herself'.

'We *do* know that he went through with the mission, don't we?' Asked Aesma Daeva, his words piercing through the cigar smoke.

'What we *do* know for sure is that the target went down, which is what matters really; but, there were four shots; two of them came from Ms. Walker's position which effectively hit the target in the heart area; the other two which came from Mr. Moone's hit a bystander in the face, and the Target's neck. I find that very interesting to say the least'.

'So now this Mr. Moone has become a Target himself'. Said Aesma Daeva as Baphomet sat across him flipping through the file papers amidst upwards spirals of thick smoke.

'Well, the reason why he became a Target was because about three to four months ago, we don't know exactly when, he travelled to Egypt, to Alexandria to be precise, not only to smuggle and sale our product, but to establish a new connection of distributors in the region. He carried eleven kilos of pure, untouched merchandise, worth millions and along with Mr. Bayard, contacted a regional link to a vast distribution circuit in the east. What happened there we don't know exactly, yet. But what we do know is that the morning after, both men were seen exiting the Royal Hotel together; hours later Mr Bayard's body was found inside his car, parked by the side of the road; a huge crater in his forehead tells us that the shot was made from a very, very short distance, in other words, from the passenger sit. Needless to say Mr. Moone nor the suitcase were anywhere to be found. We got ahold of him that same night of course, on his way back to Miami; later on he was to travel to San Francisco to get more details about the Vladimir clean up'.

'So where is the suitcase?'

'Well, here is where it gets tricky. Obviously it is to be assume that he came back from Alexandria to Miami Beach, where he resides, with the suitcase. A few days later he flies to San Francisco as directed, then to Lima to meet with Ms. Walker. We assumed that he had left the suitcase in his apartment, so while he was in Lima we went and searched, exhaustively, his place. Nothing was found. Then of course, we searched his restaurant,'

'His restaurant?'

'Yes, his restaurant, it's called…' Baphomet licked the tip of his finger to flip back some pages.

'Oh, yes here it is, it's called the Ocean Porch, right on Ocean Drive in Miami Beach.' Aesma Daeva remained in silence and his expression serious.

'Continue'.

'We found nothing there either, so we waited for his return. Once in Miami we kept him under surveillance and followed him around, we saw him with Ms. Walker having midday drinks at a little restaurant; then they headed to the Lowes Hotel, where after a couple of hours he came out and took a cab, back to his house. It was then when we saw him carrying the suitcase. He headed back to the Lowes where a while later, around thirty minutes, he came back down again, with no suitcase, and gets in his car across the street, apparently waiting for someone. While he waited we moved in, took him and the car with us'.

Aesma Daeva moved in his chair uncomfortably as the story went on, behind him the sky kept getting darker and a light drizzle starting hitting the life-size window. Baphomet related how in a desolated and abandoned warehouse they tortured Timothy Moone, whom after much pain and blood, told them that he had left it in Lara Walker's suite. Some time later when they returned to the hotel, the suite with the number given by Mr. Moone was empty, when they checked under what name was it registered, it gave an unknown name. Now they were after Lara Walker.

'But before the hunt for Ms. Walker began,' Baphomet continued. 'Mr. Moone's corpse was thrown into the ocean. For a while she managed to hide and move from place to place with much success, then we found out she was in Atlanta, where in no time we got ahold of her. She, along with a relative of hers, were trying to get rid of the merchandise, the young man, her cousin I believe, boasted out loud about it and that was the red flag we needed to pinpoint them'.

'I'm afraid you're going to tell me she didn't have the suitcase with her'.

'Oh she had the suitcase alright, but it seemed that our friend Mr. Moone had outsmarted her, and consequently us, and had traded its contents for baby powder'.

Aesma Daeva's face remained fixed with the same expression: continual thinking. As if he was thinking and imagining the story at the same time, maybe trying to look for flaws in it, something that his righthandman might be missing, or perhaps, he was trying to think like Timothy Moone or maybe Lara Walker; or could it be that he was pondering on what would he had done instead? His ice-blue eyes stared at Baphomet and at nothingness at the same time, he seemed as if he wasn't even breathing, then he said:

'Did you get rid of her?' His lips did not seemed to have even parted.

Baphomet, with exquisite manners as he had, pressed down and slowly turned the cigar stub out in the large crystal ashtray, then leaned back and cross legged as he sat, told him the real reason of his presence there.

'No, we did not get rid of her, for she's taking care of a problem thought to be solved'.

Aesma Daeva blinked once, slow and furiously. 'Which problem would that be?'

'There have been reliable accounts that Mr. Moone was 'strolling' believe it or not, through Miami Beach'.

'But you just said his *corpse* was thrown into the ocean'.

'I know I did, and I also didn't believe it when I was informed, but then I saw this photograph'. He handed him a 6x5 photo of Timothy Moone, looking like a bum, taken a few days prior.

'How do you explain this?'

'I don't, I just react. And I've reacted'. He handed him a new file on Lara Walker, detailing her day-by-day movements and progress.

'Why is *she* taking care of this?' Said him, as he flipped through.

'Well, they were involved romantically, not long ago, but it didn't work out, in fact, it turned out catastrophic for them. I'm sure she blames Mr. Moone for what happened to her. Love, sometimes, can turn into venom, of the worst kind'. He let off a single chuckle.

'I see, so that pretty much takes care of our problem'. He said closing the file and hurling it on top of the desk.

'I'm afraid we have a bigger problem now'. Said Baphomet.

The deep and far away groan of the sky announced the dense turbulence of the evening to come; great lightning and heavy downpour were about to let loose their best elements with their respective natural orchestrations.

The coldness of the apartment felt soothing and relieving from the implacable humidity that sticks to and clogs every pore of one's skin. Inside, Lara -or Alicia- immediately and unconsciously scanned the premises and thought of its contents and decoration of a 'girly type'. Francis offered a drink eventhough there was no alcohol in the apartment, Alicia declined but a shower would certainly do her good, she said, a long and hot shower, if she didn't mind.

Finally the sky stopped its growling threat and let the heavy waters come down. Francis stood in front of the balcony's door, and through the glass, the night stared back at her. The muffled sound of the falling rain on the other side of the glass numbed her as the outlines of her watery reflection took the shape of someone that wasn't her, someone else, a man, Timothy.

In the shower Lara wanted to cry but couldn't. She wanted to scream but the urge was contained and suppressed; another crack within her became larger and deeper; another faultline carved the inner outlines of a structure about to collapse. No matter how much sand and dirt washed away, she didn't feel clean, they had taken her soul somehow. Did she really believed there was such a thing as a soul? Once, many years ago the subject of souls came about in a conversation, when asked about it she responded: 'The belief in an immortal soul would imply the belief of the existence of eternal life, since I don't believe anything is truly immortal or eternal, not even the universe, therefore I can't seem to accept the idea of an immortal soul'. But there was something definitely missing inside of her, there was a void, an abyss, dark and seemingly endless. She tried to cry but she couldn't. Maybe the falling water were her tears after all, but they felt warm she thought; her tears had always been cold. The front bangs of her chopped-up-died-blonde melange of a hairdo ended where her, once deep and luring, round black eyes rested shut.

Just before the sun rose, Timothy awoke and stared into the purplelish horizon out of the windowless window. The sky appeared thin and relieved, while the air, thick and muggy, felt dragging and at times stagnant. He was consciously waiting for the sun to rise, and with this thought in mind, he remembered someone accurately commenting on the fallacy of the sun rising or setting, for although we are certain that the sun does neither nor, we consciously still referred to them as truths. And this philosophical observation was perhaps the last trace of a lost artistic feature of his relative earlier days, since his life had been severely torned by the before-and-after- awakening-at-the-beach divide.

Where the voices had ceased to torment, puzzlement and a sense of urgency had already taken over, overwhelming him so much to the point where the first sprouts of fear were felt throughout his heart. He now found himself immobile, sitting, head tilted down, on the dilapidated mattress, worn out from long use or maybe because of no use at all. In his otherwise empty doorless room, Babeuf stood in the archway appearing to be both empathetic and admiring towards Timothy.

'You realize,' He said stepping ever closer to him, while Timothy remained in the same position. 'that the signs of your coming are everywhere.' For the first time Timothy lifted his head.

'What signs?' He barely said.

'Don't you see? Everywhere in the world there's a revival of Religion, of Faith. We're getting stronger, you see, Religion is no longer the opium of the masses, but the vitamin for the weak.'

Timothy stood and approached Babeuf, their faces, a few inches apart, were at the same level. One with his blue hairs undone and his lost eyes searching, the other with his long black hair pulled back into a pony tail and his eyes full of excitement. The other held the one by the shoulders and with the last breath of authority invested in him, for he was convinced that the man in front of him was indeed the One, spoke to him what would be the last words Timothy would hear from him:

'Just say what your heart says when your heart says it, that shall be the New Word'. And at that instant, after seeing those words travel from Babeuf's lips into his ears, through his brain and down into his heart; he, Timothy, who from that moment on would no longer recognized himself as Timothy Moone, felt as light as a bubble and as blind as a bat, and suddenly he found himself alone in the middle of nothing. It wasn't dark nor bright, there was no color, no scent, it was nothingness, but he felt, for the first time, happiness. Happy in the sense that the urgency of that endless searching that had fueled his life and actions had tracelessly disappeared, that the shadow of failure which inhabited his heart since before he learnt how to speak had sudden and painlessly been evicted. He saw himself now as the Prophet of God, and carrier of the New Word.

While Timothy lost his old and found his new self in his hallucinatory revelation, Lara inspected her gun strapped in its holster. The couch is not always the most comfortable place to sleep, but when one is tire, as Lara certainly was, anywhere will do. But now she felt refreshed and focus; finding and eliminating Timothy was the goal of the day. What she thought about Timothy was as irrelevant and fundamental as what she felt for him. Since she had met him, what seemed now a long, long time ago, she hadn't really stopped thinking about him, but her personality and protective nature imposed on her the notion, that it could have been a mere temporary adolescent-type crush; but maybe it wasn't, maybe it was a little deeper than that. Anyhow, she didn't spent much time dwelling over it for she wanted to believe that by accomplishing her mission she will be out of the clutches of The

Order, as Baphomet had said. Even when she realized that she wasn't the same, that she had been wounded at the soul, she looked towards restarting her life, a completely different life in a completely different place; and that was her main concern. What Timothy was doing was of no, or little, importance to her, and the reason why he had become a Target, Lara attributed, with no doubt in her heart, to the damn suitcase that had cost her dearly: a crippled spirit and physical torment; and as she checked, cocked and locked her gun she thought that there was some kind of just retribution in her mission.

In the bedroom Francis hadn't been able to sleep through most of the night because of the thought of seeing Timothy again. And it was this ambiguous expectation that didn't give her consciousness a break longer than ten minutes, causing her to wake intermittently every so often to turn and toss, sit up and lay down again, turn the TV on and off and pass out to awake minutes later and do this over again; the uncomfort of love cannot be relieved with a sleeping pill.

The two women with one thing in common had breakfast and quickly got ready to go to the place where, according to Alicia, Timothy would most likely be found.

Order Out of Chaos

And when they found Timothy down on the floor on his knees with his head and arms hanging down, the young women of the congregation lifted him up and cleansed his face with a warm wet towel. In that instant, he awoke from his deep stupor and addressed them without fully opening his eyes: 'I have seen the future and I've left it behind'. To this the young women let go of him and fell to their knees as well for they knew God was sending his message through him. His eyes were of a certain unidentified hue, his hair bright blue seemed longer and alive, his complexion almost asiatic yellow; his lips seemed dried but the words were certainly fluid and intoxicating, but most importantly, the red fleshy scar on his forehead had grown bigger and rounder, it shone its divine light. Now, three more women and two males had come into the room and gotten on his knees in front of him. 'And from this moment on,'. He began once again, this time standing. 'all of you will be impregnated with the New Word and you will tell your children that they're no longer weak and alone for our Father is fighting with the sword of fire the infidels and conspirators of a God-less world order'.

Soon the room was filled not only with words and visions, but with men, women and children all on their knees all over the second floor, down the staircase and living room, others were outside inviting bypassers to come in and listen to the New Word; to which some would shy away but many would find it curious and amusing as they came in, enlightening and luring the longer they listened, and irresistible and enchanting as they tried to push their way through the crowd clogging the staircase in order to put a face to those sweet and authoritative words coming from the second floor. At this point is when Francis Green and Lara Walker -or Alicia Rommel- arrived at the old house after following directions from a wrinkled pink flyer; one had decided to sport sweatpants, tanktop and snickers, the other had no choice but to wear yesterday's suit, jacket included, and heels.

Lugano, Switzerland

The early morning hours weren't as cold as she thought they might be, in fact, under the sunlight, where she sat, she could feel the relentless warmth struggling to be. Patricia Echevarria had actually moved over to the only chair that was out of the shade when Mr. Sentiero, her History teacher at the Swiss Italian University, joined her at the tiny circular table of the Cafe by the side of the lake. He made a comment about the weather and the landscape, and although it was a bit chilly under the shade, most of the tables of the Cafe seemed occupied. They sat looking at the sleepy lake and the traffic of people strolling in and out of the Piazza Reforma, which seemed too busy for that time of day. Perhaps it was because it was Tuesday, and the local market displayed its freshest produce, perhaps it was simply because it was the season when the rich came down to take some time off and relax.

Two double espressos broke the ice. First, the conversation took an academical tone, with grades and exams and semesters as the main topics; gradually it turned into a current events dialog where Mr. Sentiero subtly looked for Patty's opinion on the Middle East, American Foreign

Policy, Corruption in Latin American Governments and so on. Patty, or Miss Echevarria, as he referred to her, expressed her opinions with determination and commitment, there was no vacillation in her answers and suggestions. Then Mr. Sentiero went on to talk a bit about himself: he began with a brief description of his childhood in Milano and then his studies in various european universities. Both his parents were diplomats working for their respective governments, his mother was Italian, his father Swiss. He himself had inherited the look from the mother's side and the thought process from the father's. Actually his father wanted him to be involve in government matters but he decided he was more incline towards academia than politics; anyway, he thought, these two intertwine often, or at least they're supposed to.

Patty just listened as Mr. Sentiero shared his concise biography with her, but somehow she knew there was something special about this revelation, for he was no ordinary History teacher; at forty-five he was regarded an eminence in the university and scholarly circles around Europe, he had worked side by side with several Presidents, Prime Ministers and Chancellors; and the way he taught his academic subject was more like revealing a more interesting history of how History came to be; in all, she not only had respect and admiration for him but a certain intellectual awe as well.

'Ms.Echevarria, the reason why I'm sharing with you all this,' Said Mr. Sentiero. 'is because you have certain qualities that separate you from the others in your class; you have intelligence, motivation and determination. Theses qualities were found in myself when I was about your age, and I was asked to join, just as my parents had before me, a group of selected people, very special people indeed, with special capacities and motivation to shape, or re-shape, our social realities worldwide; now, I would like to ask you to come to this meeting, so you can understand, in more depth what I'm trying to tell you.' He handed her a card and she held and stared at it for the rest of the conversation. 'Tonight, at eight o'clock sharp. When you arrive there just show them the card and get inside, I'll be there waiting for you'. Patty remained with her stare locked onto the card in her hand.

Having payed the check he got up and taking his leather briefcase he addressed her one last time: 'I know I don't have to tell you this but, please keep the utmost discretion about this meeting, this information is meant exclusively for you Miss Echevarria; I will see you tonight'.

After finishing her secondary studies in a private school in Lima, Patricia Echevarria was sent to Switzerland for her higher education. Her mother, Anais, was being convinced to run for Senate by her husband Jose Carlos, who had been a Senator himself, and was now evaluating the possibilities of running for President in a near future. As they were planning and working towards their new goals, across the Atlantic, Patty headed to the address printed on the card with a thousand thoughts and emotions coming and going and often stumbling upon each other.

On the outside it seemed as a large residence in the style of a country cottage. She walked a lengthy path sided by sleeping flowers and rustling trees. She sensed jazmin as the pervasive scent of welcome. At the doorsteps she handed, as told, the card given to her and she was let in. Her coat was taken by another butler and a glass of champagne was immediately offered. She took one of the ten glasses that stood proud on the silver tray, held in front of her by yet another white-gloved steward. The soft melodies of Bellini were as pervasive as the scent of jazmin. She was dressed in long fitted black pants, leather boots, and beige cashmere sweater. Mr. Sentiero hadn't given her any specifics regarding attire but she looked fine; and that's exactly what he said behind her.

'Thanks, by my first impression for a minute I thought I was underdressed'. She said referring to the house and the butlers and music.

'Well, as you might noticed, most of the people here are men'.

And as soon as he said that, Patty scanned the place for women and found only one, talking to a group of men.

'And why is that?' She turned to him.

'Because very few women take interest in ruling the world'. He said with a smile that turned to laughter. She laughed thinking he was right.

Later they were all announced that the meeting was about to take place. Mr. Sentiero guided her through wide and long halls, sided with mirrors and paintings, illuminated by a series of crystal chandeliers all the way to an auditorium that sat maybe, four hundred people. All the chairs, after twenty minutes of influx of people, were occupied.

A number of people came up to the podium to speak, in different languages, about the state of affairs of the world: the potential for the wars to come, globalization and unification, the new drug policy, the importance of intervention and the dangers of military regimes in South America, Africa, and Asia. Patricia up to this point, althought thankful to have attended such meeting, was a bit disappointed at the lack of real insight about world affairs; what she'd heard so far was people pointing the benefits of some policies and the problems of some countries but nothing substantial, to her this was another political get-together; then everyone fell silent all of the sudden. A man walked in from the side of the podium and the whole place bursted in applauses. Patty didn't know what was going on, and when she was about to ask her teacher, everyone stood, still applauding, louder now, at the man standing before them, in a blue suit, with ice-blue eyes.

'Listen'. Said Mr. Sentiero without looking at her.

Patty took a look around, everyone's gaze seemed fixed on this man; obviously all the other speakers where just the appetizers, this one was the one they had been waiting for.

He cleared his throat and took a sip of water. The silence was so severe that Patty thought she'd heard the liquid gulped down his throat.

'Many of you know me, for those of you who don't, I am the head of The Order, an organization whose sole mission, is to unite the world'. A roar of applauses bursted again. Patty looked around again and it was the same: no one talked, no one looked around. 'As we have heard, there is still a long and bumpy road ahead of us, but the light at the end is shinning brighter; people are slowly just beginning to open their eyes, to see what might lie beyond their noses; for that's how blind we are, that's how blind we've been; for hundreds, for thousands of years; but that's all about to change'.

Patty wasn't looking around anymore, she wasn't just hearing another speaker talk, she felt that she was witnessing imminent change.

'But change takes courage, change takes time, change, sometimes, take lives; but, most important of all, change takes knowledge; and the will, to choose knowledge over fear, knowledge over faith, knowledge over God'.

The applauses were uplifting, their energy was tangible.

'The great catastrophes in History, have been committed over the wrong ideals, the wrong perceptions, the wrong beliefs. History tends to repeat itself, from the grand to the micro, the same ideals seem to resuscitate every so often. But like I've said: that's all about to change.

'Some philosophers will tell us that the choice of knowledge over God was made a long, long time ago; when Man ate the apple and traded everything he had, including immortality, for knowledge. Some other will tell us that mankind, by becoming aware of itself, thus stepping out of the animal kingdom, had chosen knowledge over blissful ignorance. Either way we've been punished eversince. What I will tell you is that, thanks to a few enlightened ones, mankind managed to survive, and evolve, and spread throughout this planet. But many forgot the objective; many became fearful, many surrendered whatever left overs they had, to the idea of God, but fortunately, many still kept the vision intact, and passed it on through the ages, all the way down to you.

'What shall we do then to change people's minds? Nothing. We know who we are, and that is our most valuable weapon. It is them, who are in the endless effort to change people's minds, to recruit souls, as they say, to convert, to transform. The only thing we transform is nature. The essence of the original Man, descendants of the First People, cannot be transformed, cannot be converted; it can be blinded, it can be put to sleep, but it can't be transformed. But those unfortunate who are, we certainly can live without; we don't need them; we don't want people whose minds can be easily changed; we don't want the weak, for the weak shall inherit death. What we want are people who have always been that way they are; people who have always thought the way they do; people who under any circumstances ever even imagined to think the way the others do; these are people of the future. These are the descendants of the first Illuminated Ones. These are the ones who will fight the Islamic cancer and the Christian brainwashing, and the religions whose sole purpose is to numb and blind. These are the ones who would wake up mankind and lead the way back to Eden, to retake immortality'.

The crowd on their feet, applauding, seem rejuvinated, radiant, contagious, loud. Patricia Echevarria clapped her hands numb way after he had gone; his words, his look; his self had overwhelmed her in such a way that she felt she had found her real self, his words had spoken to the innermost of desires in her heart. She wanted to meet him right away. Mr. Sentiero asked her to calm down first, and told her that he would be around for cocktails in the gallery.

'Let's go, I want a cocktail'. She said.

The immense gallery was large enough to hold, comfortably, the four hundred plus guests, thirtysomething butlers and a ten piece string orchestra. To her it resembled, by the tapestries on the wall, the chandeliers that glittered a million sparkles, and the marble on the floor, a Royal Ball in the Versailles of Louis XIV. She walked around, champagne flute in hand, and saw that everyone was engaged in serious conversations about this and that. Mr. Sentiero had disappeared and she felt odd, in the middle of such vastness of everything: wealth, taste, class, people, culture, conversations, ideas…then she saw him.

He also was engaged in conversation. There were three other men in front of him, listening attentive. She paused for a second to think about her approach. She didn't want to seem like a young intrusive girl, eventhough she appeared to be the youngest in this whole palace. She gulped the champagne down and took a deep breath, then, took her insecure steps towards the group of gentlemen across the room. As she approached the music kept getting louder; she was unsure and determined at the same time; and she stopped right behind one of the men. They all immediately turned to her. She looked straight and there he was.

'Excuse me, gentlemen…' She swallowed and address him. 'I…I just wanted to…congratulate you for your speech'. They all had sympathetic smiles on their faces. He just stared at her as if he was trying to recognize her.

'Do I know you miss…'

'Echevarria'. She replied. 'Patricia Echevarria'.

'Well, I'm so glad you're here, do you live in Lugano?'

'Well, I am attending the university here, I'm from Lima, Peru'. He was scrutinizing her with his fixed stare, and she knew it.

'Are you related to Senator Jose Carlos Echevarria'. She smiled proudly.

'That would be my father'.

'I see'. He said nothing else while she was waiting for a more extensive comment.

'Do you know him?'

'Personally, no, I haven't had the pleasure, but I've heard a lot about him'. She noticed her time was up.

'Well, I'm sorry for having interrupted your conversation gentlemen, nice to meet you again…sir, hope I'll get to listen to another speech of yours again…' She said retreating.

'I'm sure *I'll* hear from you again, Ms. Echevarria'.

And with that Patricia Echevarria had found what she was looking for, a reason, an ideal to do what others chose not to. To intervene in the affairs of her country and make History happen not just watch it being made by the inadequate and incapable. From that point on, she would be the relentless impulse for mother to run for Senate, and the quiet voice in her father's head to consider the Presidency. And as far as her, she had bigger plans for her.

Gino Gianoli

The crowd outside the old house was going berserk. Francis hesitated when Lara suggested to push their way through. There were people in tears: they seemed happy and sad, frightened and brave; they seemed insane, hypnotized, scary.

'What is this place Alicia, some kind of cult?' She yelled at her as they squeezed through people coming in and out, screaming and repeating the words passed on from person to person, like a game of telephone.

'We've got to find Timothy, look around! he's got to be here somewhere.' Suddenly, people and more people got in between them and Francis lost sight of Alicia. Being in that living room was more like being in a concert, in General Admission: people were sweaty, smelly, rubbing and pushing as more tried to make their way up the clogged staircase. Some of them wore regular clothes, some others wore rags and tunics. Francis couldn't see the entrance anymore, she kept shoving herself forward looking for an open space.

Meanwhile, Lara had reached the patio, where the dried and grassless yard was finally stamped out by the feet of the faithful. There was a large crowd there as well, but no where as tight as in the living and dining room. She tried to ask the people there what was going on, why so much commotion, but none seemed to acknowledge her presence, they were whispering words really fast, like a hurried, memorized prayer. She lifted her head over the others to try to find Francis, but with no luck. Then decided to go back into the house, through the pandemonium, and try to make it upstairs. She took a few deep breaths of fresh air for she was going to need them, that's when she heard the strange man's voice .

'You came to see him as well'. She looked at him and then around her, she wasn't sure whether he was talking to her or someone behind her.

'Excuse me, do I know you?' He took a couple steps closer. She got on guard.

'Not exactly but I know why you're here. You need to see him. It's a matter of life or death isn't it?

Lara didn't know what to say. In front of her stood this tall, handsome man, clean and well articulated.

'What are you talking about?' She looked into his deep black eyes that reminded her own eyes how they used to be.

'Come with me, I'll take you to him'. And with that he turned and walked away. She stood there a few seconds of hesitation, then decided to follow.

Through a backdoor they went up a narrow makeshift stairwell made out of old wood and rusted metal bars, that squeaked and swayed, and seemed about to collapse any minute now.

'I'm looking for Timothy Moone'. Said her as they reached second floor, still doubting whether it was a good idea to follow this guy around this nuthouse. The man held the door open for her.

'I know who you're looking for'. He closed it behind her.

Surrounded by almost thirty people in this tiny room, The Prophet didn't feel the least bit claustrophobic, there were at least a hundred more by the hall, down the stairs, in the living room, the patio, and outside in the front of the house, The Prophet spoke loud and clear, commanding and advising; warning about the days to come.

'The New Word is a call to war,' He announced, some people with their eyes closed felt the words like flames shooting into their hearts, some others with their gaze fixed on the holy sign in his forehead. 'a war against the rulers of this world whose ultimate goal is to legally unite the world, this way their order and control would be more efficient and much faster'.

He kept speaking to the crowd; the crowd then repeated his words to the ones in the back, they would go on and do the same to the ones standing in the stairwell, and so on. The Prophet felt the effervescence of his soul spilling through his mouth, that warm eternal light that elevated him above all others present, that eternal truth that had, once again, evolved into something else, something new; the New Word.

'The New Word is not about waiting for the appearance of the spirit of God, it will instead create it from scratch, new and stronger, revitalized for another thousand years'. What the Prophet was trying to say was that the New Word, which meant the New Way, was going to virtually destroy the old teachings and impose a new, more fresh, and attractive teaching. Religion, as he put it, have decayed so badly that what was seen as the source of all virtue, was now seen as the reason why people killed themselves and others, it was the reason why wars really never ended, it was the reason why there's so much poverty in the world; all because

Religion has lost its vision, its relevance, its miracles. It has been fighting itself instead of adapting to the new realities. It had stood by the old teachings when new ones were required for a new understanding of the world and God. It has eaten its own children and vomit them again. Religion has become an endangered species and was not helping itself survive. The Order, for more than two thousand years now, had been waiting for this moment, and they were working fast and hard to accelerate its final fall. More and more atrocities will be committed in the name of Religion, more and more people will die in its name, and more, much more, will ask for its persecution and control and eventual annihilation.

The Prophet spoke of the New Truth; and how this Truth would lead to transformation, the ultimate transformation of Faith. The enchanted listeners felt the renewal and strengthening of their soul; for many years now the link to the one-God have been progressively deteriorating, and the weak had become ever weaker and worse of all, they've felt abandoned by their God. The people listened with their hearts and minds to the one who would lead them to reconquer the world, but suddenly, his mesmerizing eloquence did not feel the same; as he turned his head he saw something that disturbed his thoughts and consequently his speech; something that dragged him back down to earth and made him feel lost, guilty, small, happy, frightened: human; something that hit the only string, the only link to his previous life: these were two large, round eyes staring at him, they were pitch black and mind-wrecking; it was Lara standing there, with her screaming yellow hair, in a pin stripe dark-blue woman suit, with her hand crawling into the side of the jacket.

Francis hadn't stop sweating since she was swallowed by the mass of people pushing and shoving around the house. She knew that Alicia had to be upstairs since she had been bouncing around the rest of the house; but how did she managed to get up there when there were maybe fifty people trying to go up and down, most of them stuck there? She must've found a way, she thought. To her, Alicia seemed like the aggressive type that didn't wait for things to happen, instead, she would make them happen. She thought about this and asked herself what kind of woman was she? How many times had she had the things that she wanted come true? How many times did she go after them to make them come true? Why was she thinking all this now? She heard people repeating messages to the ones behind and these in turn would do just the same, like a loud secret being told, coming from the people upstairs, down to where she stood, all the way outside to the street. Since everyone talked, and others repeated the same words, and still some others would be crying or praying, the place was very loud indeed. Francis tried to listen to the words spoken from mouth to mouth, and as she heard them repeating it, before, around and past her, she thought she would faint.

'He won't forget us twice'. The people said over and over.

The hall was crowded of course, but Lara and the strange man guiding her, slipped through with relative easiness. He lighted a cigarette as they walked, offered one but she was in no mood to smoke.

'Thanks, I quit'.

Up there the people were louder and in a deeper trance. She turned to him and noticed his clean appearance and mysterious aura, his long black hair, pulled into a ponytail, shined healthy and alive.

'By the way what's your—? She was going to ask but he had already spoken.

'I know you have come to kill him'. She stopped in her tracks and immediately, her right hand could feel, through the fabric of her jacket, the cold steel of her gun.

'What the fuck are you?' Now it was his turn to stop.

Sometimes destiny makes you be who you are, sometimes destiny is what you will become, but there are other times when one, realizing who he is and projecting to what he wishes to become, creates destiny. Lara always knew who she was and what she didn't want to be, but she never could figured out what she wanted to accomplish for herself. But the vivid memory of that old dark warehouse, the putrid smell of burnt flesh with vintage cigar, the plastic handcuffs slicing her wrists, while her naked body, covered in white powder, laid face down on the concrete floor and the endless penetrations that ripped her insides apart, one after another, after another, after another, tearing her thick armor into irredeemable pieces, caused her swift hand to unlock, cock and shoot the strange man right in the middle of his forehead, as he was turning to her. His head snapped backwards pulling his body along to land flat, with open arms, on that old and dusty wooden floor.

The shot was hardly heard, thanks to the silencer, always attached to her gun, but the graceful fall and deep thump was seen and felt by everyone around; by the time they approached the body Lara was gone.

A dark empty room, tiny and smelly, served as her hideout; as she looked closer it turned out to be a bathroom. The voices outside didn't seemed to have change their rhythm; there were no screams or noises of people running, but there was a voice, a particular voice amongst a hundred that sounded more than familiar, intimate. That voice came from the room adjacent to where she hid. Without thinking she ventured out and saw that the entrance was completely blocked by a mob of people that extended from the room all the way to down the stairs, from where she thought she heard the name Alicia being called, she immediately thought of Francis, but when she looked they were all the same crazy cult idiots climbing onto each other to get to the top; she turned back towards the hall and to her surprise the body wasn't there anymore. She decided to push her way into the room. As she moved forward the voice was no only intimate but was sweet as well, it was soothing and strong. She kept squeezing her slim body through, pushing and being pushed, until finally she reached the front line. Her perception was as disturbing as it was pitiful: Timothy stood on a skinny mattress in the far corner of the overcrowded and foul room, his blue hairs longer than ever and messy as always, his face thinner and whiter, he appeared to haven't shaved in weeks; a round scar on his forehead, large and pronounced; his body covered by a filthy and raggedy bedspread giving her the impression that she stood in front of a malnourished shaman heavily influenced by the Punk scene. She felt pity and tenderness towards him, who stood there, insane, speaking beautiful but meaningless words; that weird, existentialist killer that had made her feel very special and flattered, but also confused and scared, and because of him, tormented for the rest of her days. Her hand reached inside her jacket heading once more for the shoulder holster. As he spoke, his eyes looked at everyone and no one, that is, until they stopped on hers.

She saw the entrance and thought about giving up this stupid, and useless, and scary search. Francis was eight feet from the door where they came in and still, she calculated, it would take her another five minutes to actually get there. People kept popping in and the heat was getting hazardously high. She saw the way out and thought about how Alicia had never told her why did she think Timothy would be in here, with all these lunatics? Who was she anyway? She certainly didn't *look* like a detective. Like a drugged out detective, maybe. And where did she go? She saw the stairwell packed with people like sardines, and then she saw the exit. What the hell was she doing here anyways? She turned to the stairs once again and screamed Lara's detective name out loud. Sweat was dripping from her forehead and claustrophobia lurked around the corner. She tried again. *Alicia!* But nothing. She then decided whatever energies were left in her, be used to make it to the outside, and so she did.

As she made it out of the house tears started streaming down, as fast as her legs ran, with anger and desperation; the valve had been opened and the flowing wouldn't stop until the reservoir of her heart was left empty and dry. The tears carried in them the impotence of having the strength and not using it, the anger at one's self for letting love slip by; they carried blame and fear; fear of change, fear of lost, and all the other things that Francis Green could've done and say but didn't have the guts to.

She ran for miles, the tears were the fuel, the restaurant was the refuge. Her legs wouldn't stop until they had taken her back into her little world; her wavy blonde hair floated behind her while the hope for Timothy travelled in front, like the toy rabbit for the dogs at the track, so close but always a bit faster.

And suddenly he became quiet. Silence took long enough to cause discomfort among the listeners who started looking around and whispering to each other back and forth, always observant of his every move. The Prophet seemed lost in her gaze and there was no movement. Lara felt how gradually people began moving away from her, her eyes shifted, left, right, fast and continuously while her finger became tighter on the trigger. The Prophet took a small step forward and dropped the bedspread from his body, displaying the many bruises and scars scattered all over his torso and arms. 'Love is like life,' He shattered the silence, startling some. 'it is diverse, it is mysterious, it is immortal'. A semicircle had formed around Lara leaving the open space for him. He kept getting closer. Some women were praying, others were crying, others were just in awe. 'Do you know what Yahweh's secret was in order for him to take absolute control over the other gods?' He kept getting closer and the room hotter. Lara felt suffocation lurking around the corner. 'Do you know Lara, my love?' He asked louder and the people whispered to others: doyouknowlaramylove? doyouknowlaramylove? doyouknowlaramylove? and the others whispered to others: doyouknowlaramylove? Lara looked around her and held her breath staring at his eyes. His eyes weren't the same. She remembered playful, naughty eyes; these were tormented, twisted. He took another step forward but her gun was already pointing blank at him. The circle around them immediately opened up.

She pointed the gun at him and all around, just in case someone gets any holy ideas of martyrdom. The crowd was scared, some just stepped back and took off, some didn't dared to move, some prayed, and some sounded outraged at the fact that she was threatening The Prophet.

'Get back!' Screamed Lara to the people around her.

'I'll tell you what his secret was'. Said The Prophet.

'You're insane Timothy, and you're going to die'.

'It was life! his secret was life!'.

'Good bye Timothy, I curse the day I ever met you'. Her gun pointed directly at his forehead, at the holy sign from where his inspiration came from. The tip of the silencer stood fifteen inches from him.

'The God of Life rises, from the death of the other gods'. As soon as his lips pronounced these words, Timothy the Prophet saw a flash, an explosion, a burst of light, white and yellow, that blinded him for a thousand years; then, it got dark and quiet. The eternal dreamless sleep fell upon him.

As soon as the bullet broke through his skull, creating a small dark-red dot inside the larger round scar in his forehead and a bigger one on the back, everyone snapped; then began the screaming and crying, the moaning and chaos. Still pointing her gun she walked out of the room, down the stairs, where the mob of people parted like the Red Sea, and out the door.

Upstairs in the room, the crowd gathered around their Prophet. Some on their knees, some standing; they all watched as the puddle of blood expanded from underneath his head. His eyes still opened stared at the ceiling while his dry lips seemed to pronounce the word *'life'* from within himself. A few began chanting the old songs, and some more followed along, but these ones contained the words that had been spoken: the New Word.

Lara Walker rode a cab back to her dingy motel room by the airport. Took a fast shower, her gun closed by, changed and picked up her luggage: one medium size sports bag. She checked for the plane ticket and it was there. Took another cab and twenty minutes later, she was checking in at the counter. She had come right on time, the counter attendant said, the plane was being boarded now. Aisle or window? Window she said, so when the plane lowered below the clouds, she would be able to see Greece from above.

Gino Gianoli

Miami Beach, U.S.

And so he waited. Inside his car Timothy Moone was having second thoughts about the nature of his recent actions, especially this one. What was he trying to proof himself? The day had been perfect so far: the bloodymarys, the long conversation, that soft and intense kiss…followed by his passionate bites and her creamy screams; the sweetest sweat of their bodies streaming to the east and west, from one mouth, through the steamy landscapes of the bodies, to another mouth, and back; then, the soothing bath…the cooling blue sky…and the whirlingly curious seabreeze, freeflowing in through the great terrace doors, estimating the damage done. What was he trying to accomplish? Now, he sat uncomfortably in his car outside the Hotel waiting for her to walk or not to walk out of there, to leave or not to leave with him. The day was too beautiful to ruin it with insecurities. He looked at his watch; twenty minutes had past since he came down, if she was to make a run for it, it should be right about now, he thought. But why should we test that ones we love? Why not? Doesn't God tests our love and faith all the time? Timothy Moone wasn't skilled at solving dilemmas of the heart. Instead he thought about calling Francis back, to let her know that he was alright, that he'd been back in town, but there was something he just had to take care of; whatever else he would say to her depended totally on the outcome of this event. If Lara walked out of the Hotel, with the suitcase, then he'd realized that she wasn't the one for him; that she hadn't hesitated to doublecross him; but on the other hand, if she didn't come down in the next five minutes, he'd run up there, all the way to the penthouse, and hopefully find her packed and ready to leave with him. The suitcase would either make her run or help her make up her mind. Timothy hoped for the latter of course. He looked at his watch again, in three minutes it'd all be over. Then, he heard a knock on his window.

After the tempestuous love making they had jumped into the milky white bathtub, more for fun than a break; eventhough both were exhausted, they were also renewed, and soon, submerged in peach-scented bubbles. Later, as they laid, wet and naked, sniffing coke on the bed, Timothy would go on to openly express his desire to quit the lifestyle and what he thought was a mutual feeling. Lara, being caught off guard, in so many words replied that, he was jumping to conclusions way too fast. Far from being discouraged, he thought he had one last trick up his sleeve. Quickly dressing, he tells her that he would be right back.

'Don't you dare go anywhere, beautiful'. He runs out the door, down the elevator and into a cab. As it pulled out of the main entrance, he turns to see that cylindrical tall white building that contained his only chance at love.

Back at his house, he ran to the kitchen, where in one of the lower cabinets, a secret compartment laid hidden. From there he took a black leather suitcase and a blue sportsbag. He carefully unlocked one and unzipped the other, pulling out to the side of each, eleven thick bundles tightly wrapped in a special type of white elastic material, which was weightless, impermeable and unflammable. He attentively switched the packets from one to the other, closed them and proceeded to place the sportsbag back into the secret compartment. As he stepped out the door the phone rang. He paused and turned. He let it ring until the machine picked it up.

> 'Hi Timothy it's Francis, just wanted to see if you were back or...not. Um, if I'm not mistaking you were supposed to be here almost a week ago, and this must be the hundredth message that I leave on your machine, thought it musta been full by now. (laugh)
>
> Well, I'm worried, I miss you...(silence)

The restaurant is doing fine, but I'm not. Hope you haven't forgot about me...please call and say that you're fine, please?

By the way, I had to fire Serge, he tried to steal money from the Bar bank, and now we know who opened those safes, who would've thought ha?. But, if you wanna know more you're gonna have to call mister.

Call soon. Or I'll try again. Bye. I...I miss you'. Click.

Her voice was the same, he thought: sweet, undemanding, loving. He made an attempt at reaching the phone and calling her back, but the weigh in his hand reminded him of another woman. He paused, thought about it, and turned around. He closed and locked the door behind him -and that would be the last time he'd ever see his house. Hurried to his car, door was unlock, he'd never left the door unlock in his short existence, but there was no time for that now. Tires peeled off towards Collins Avenue and 15th street. On his way there, self-consciousness started kicking in, he began by wondering whether what he was about to do was the right thing. But his head was still too hot and any moral or philosophical questions quickly evaporated; what really mattered to him, was that he had found love. He was completely convinced about it, from the moment he saw her at the steakhouse in Lima, he knew she was it. What Timothy Moone felt was something that only a few can identified with; and those few lucky ones would've done the same thing.

He had parked across the street looking straight ahead at the exit ramp of the Lowes. He walked through the lobby, zig-zagging a bunch of people, until he reached the elevator. Inside, he stared at his reflection, front and sides, and he seemed anxious, thirsty, careless, childish. He didn't quite recognized himself, his conscious spoke again: 'take it easy', it said, but it was too late.

The door wasn't locked, he stepped in. The only sound was the breeze, bringing omens from the sea. Timothy found Lara in a white terry cloth robe, her wet and long black hair was pulled back into a tail, she sat, picking with her fingers diced fresh fruit from a white bowl, facing the infinite blueness of the ocean and the sky and how they seemlessly united at the horizon. She turned to him with all the peacefulness in the world, her eyes round and black narrowed as she smilingly offered him some fruit. And this image would be ingrained not only in his mind, but in the innermost of his heart, and from this, he knew it was good.

Inside, he apologized again about what he'd said earlier, and how she was right, he was moving too fast.

'Listen Timothy,' Said Lara, sitting on the bed. 'I, I do feel something special about this, and I do want to continue it, but—'

'You don't have to say anything,' Interjected Timothy. 'I know what you mean, exactly.' But there was something else he needed to tell her, and he asked if he could confide in her.

'Of course, what is it?'

He pulled, from the side of the sofa, the black leather suitcase and laid it flat on the bed. Lara looked at it and then at him.

'What is it?'

'My future'. He said, unlocked and clicked it open.

What she saw needed no introduction, no explanation, no discussion. The neatly arranged white packets left no doubt of their imminence.

'You know what thi—'

'Yes Timothy! I think I have a pretty good guess what this is!!!' Lara immediately backed and got up, as if the contents of the suitcase were radioactive.

'What's the matter with you?'

'Please tell me it's not that…new thing! that new cocaine'. He just stood there staring at her. 'Oh my god, how did you get ahold of this? No, forget it, I don't even want to know'. She had already started to dress. Timothy held her by her arms asking her to relax, to listen to him for a second. She swung her arms releasing them from his grip.

'Listen, I'm offering you to come with me, we'll go to any country you want. With this we can live a pretty good life anywhere in the world; plus I could sell my restaurant and—'

'Timothy what are you talking about? You realize what you're asking me?'

'Yes'.

'No! You don't. You're asking me to go into hiding to another country, god knows for how long! You're asking me to leave everything behind!'

'What would you be leaving behind Lara, really?'

Silence filled the room, the seabreeze had stopped blowing for quite some time now.

Timothy picked up the white terry cloth robe and laid it carefully on top of the bed. He told her that if she didn't want to come with him, it was okay, but he was determined to leave the country and go into a comfortable hiding, once he sold the merchandise, which would be...he looked at his watch, in a couple of hours, he said.

'You already have a buyer?' Lara's eyes widened again. He told her how he got in contact with an old partner of his, a frenchman named Bernard, and how he was interested in purchasing the merchandise.

'He's a very funny guy, and very smart, you'd definitely like him'. The image of the smoking hole in Bernard's forehead flashed before his eyes. The favor that he needed was that he had to leave the suitcase here with her, for half an hour max, then he'd be back pick it up and take off.

'You think you can do that for me?' Lara remained confused and silent.

'I don't know'.

It was just going to be half an hour, he said, half an hour is nothing. Lara's usual determination had suddenly been bombarded from all sides. She thought about what she felt for him, the money that suitcase represented, the freedom that money represented, as well as the danger. She thought about her life, what would she be leaving behind, really? For how long did she think she was going to do this kind of work? How long would it take for another man to love her the way he said he did? For how long would she remain young and strong?

'Aren't you concern that the people that we work for are going to hunt you down?

She sat on the edge of the bed, Timothy squatted in front of her, holding her knees.

'They hunt only when they know who to hunt'. He said with all the calmness in the world.

'They'll find out though, I know, they always do'.

'The last link to me has vanished from this world. Now, I gotta go, I'll be back in half an hour'.

And holding her head between the palms of his hands, he kissed her forehead, his eyes closed wishing she'd make the right decision.

As he descended, he took another look at his reflection inside the elevator. The floor numbers beeped. What was he doing? asked the reflected self. He was trying to convince her to leave with him. Why did he leave the suitcase with her? Because the suitcase will reveal the real Lara Walker.

And so he waited. The day had been perfect so far. The sun was still shinning and the few clouds couldn't be any whiter. Timothy looked at his watch and thought that in three minutes he would finally know. Then, a knock on the window startled him. A man in a suit bent over, signaling him to roll it down. His muscles contracted and his heart inflated. Through the rear-view mirror he saw a white van parked behind him; to his right, on the sidewalk, another one in a suit bent looking through the passenger window; and another white van blocked his front view. The engine was on and his gun was underneath his seat, where it always was, and he thought, in that eternal fraction of a second, that he could shoot his way out. They kept knocking on the window and looking around. His left hand was still visible on the wheel while his right one made a lightning reach under the seat. His fingers searched, reaching deeper to find nothing. Nothing! He peacefully sat up, took a long and deep breath, and prepare for the most unwelcome truth. Right then, he felt the cold and ruthless tip of a gun barrel pointing, at the back of his head. 'Don't move Mr. Moone'. Said a remorseless voice from the backseat; he looked up towards the penthouse, then came the injection and the deep fall into unconsciousness.

Lara Walker sat on sofa on the right, the black suitcase rested on the sofa on the left. She stared at it uncertain, over a hexagonal coffee table, with a single flower, brochures and hotel magazines. Behind them the white linen curtains flowed wildly with the wind that hummed its song of sorrow, the sunny day of a minute ago had become grey, the white and peaceful clouds had turned dirty and angry. More than half an hour had past and he wasn't back. Half an hour is nothing, he'd said. She recounted the conversation, and how passionate he was about it. Maybe, she should leave with him, somewhere far. She thought about loving him. Had she ever loved a man before? That didn't mattered, she could certainly learn to love him. But, where the hell was he? She took another look at the suitcase; it seemed as if it talked to her, but whatever it was saying, it didn't say love, or Timothy. Lara stood and walked into the bedroom to pack her few clothes. She thought about taking off, and leaving the suitcase there; so when he'd be back, he'd get the message. With her bag in one hand and her gun strapped in the shoulder holster, she walked out of the penthouse and waited by the elevator. She didn't want to think about anything, she just wanted to get back to her normal life. The elevator arrived. Afterall, didn't she do what she do best? The doors split open. *'The last link to me had vanished from this world'* She walked inside and saw her reflection on both sides. *'They hunt only when they know who to hunt'* She pressed Lobby and stepped back. *'What would you be leaving behind Lara, really?'* And before the doors closed she stretched her left arm in between. She ran back to the penthouse, snatched the suitcase out of the sofa and took the stairwell down to the lobby, making her exit through the pool, and into the beach; where she walked on slanted sands under the threatening clouds.

The pressure of the cold water against his face shocked his eyes open jerking him out of the feeble shelter of dreams. He found himself in the most uncomfortable position after being conscious for only a minute. His feet were shackled and his hands cuffed. One hand was cuffed to the other between the two legs, underneath the shackles; thus forcing him to be in a squatting and bowing position, all the time. Now that he was awake, he realized that the reason why he was on his feet was because his neck was chained to the wall behind him, giving him enough reach to squat, but not to sit. If he'd stayed asleep for too long, he would choke. It was dark and cold and he was naked. Was he dead yet? When he heard movement and noises, he remembered what happened, and he wished he was. As the steel door opened and some light managed to slip through, the cell where he found himself, appeared more filthy that imagined, immediately the vintage stench of vomit and piss became vivid and suffocating. He, himself had urinated where he squatted.

'Well, well, well, look who we have here'. Said the man coming through the door. 'They told me and I couldn't believe it; Mr. Moone, I must say, we are deeply disappointed'.

Timothy tried to lift his head with great struggle. When the man covered in shadows moved to where there was more light, he saw the man in the Mansion, Baphomet.

'If I recall correctly, you once told me, Mr, Moone, that you were most interested in the arts. And I too, thought, after meeting you, that secretly, you fancied yourself an Artist'. He lit and puffed his cigar. Its pure and thick aroma tried to fight against the ancient stench of defecation. 'I must admit, Mr. Moone, that's the one thing we have in common: we are both frustrated artists'. Long streaks of saliva hung from the side of his mouth as the pain in his curving back became intolerable, from his nape to his tailbone. 'And as a fellow artist, I'd like to share an epiphany I had long ago'. He got closer to him, squatting so as to be at his same level, looking for his stare. He took a deep drag of the cigar, its tip glowing red, thick, and furious; then aimed it at the forehead.

'To be an artist one must know how to suffer.' He began. 'One must need and even desire to suffer. One must welcome pain'. One hand thrust the burning tip of his cigar, against Timothy's forehead while the other holding it still. He screamed and pleaded to the muted walls of torture. And as he turned it slowly, he kept sharing his revelation. 'And it is this pain, not the physical one, but the emotional, the mental, and the spiritual pain, the artist's everlasting and everflowing source of inspiration'. The burning leaves, compressed and robust, melted the first thin layers of skin melting its way to the bone.

'Now, you're going to be inspired and you'll tell me what I need to know; the burning sensation in your forehead it's just the source of that inspiration'.

Timothy Moone screamed his last screams. Pain had taken over his body, manifesting in every which way imaginable. He thought about mentally escaping, but all the doors were closed. The screams turned to words, the words formed sentences and stories. Everything he had to say and all the names he had to mention, from Vladimir Guzman, through Bernard Bayard, to Lara Walker and the suitcase, Timothy Moone make known. Baphomet finally removed the stubbed cigar out of his forehead, leaving a wide and round black circle, that appeared alive and growing. Before he fainted, knowing that if he did he would choke, he thought about her, sitting in the terrace looking at the big blue sky, her hair black, her eyes blacker.

Two weeks later, he was taken out of the cell, apparently beaten till death, and placed on a boat. This boat would take the body deep into the sea where it was to be dropped. The men in charge of this felt movement in the corpse's limbs and immediately proceeded to beat and stomp on it, every which way they could, since they weren't carrying any guns. When it got dark enough, they threw the body overboard, in a region where sharks are known to roam at that particular time. The men

Gino Gianoli

stared in darkness, following the wobbling corpse with the feeble flash lights, as it drifted further and further away. It floated slow, facing down, for longer than normal; then, it quietly sank.

New York, U.S.

This city teaches one to act, not to think. Said one to the other. The two of them remained sited as they were; outside the weather worsened as it was. And the conversation took on a solemnly tone. There had been, more than ever, continuous announcements, in the underground congregations, of the coming of their Prophet.

The Order had known about these underground groups who, long ago, broke off with their Church, Temple, and Mosque, to become self sufficient, religionless organizations. These were beginning to expand, but their numbers still remained low. Their objective was to lead a Second Reformation, not only of the Church, but of all religion, thus creating a new idea of God. In order for them to accomplish this, The Prophet, the One who shall speak the New Word, must physically appear to them and lead them towards their goal. The Order, since the discovery of their existence, had been keeping a close eye on these people, who lived in communities, often in the poor areas of the big cities. One of them had established themselves around the outskirts of Downtown Miami, their spiritual leader and financier, a one Babeuf, last name unknown, had been under their scope for quite sometime now; he was regarded in the underground circles as a mediator, a foreseer, who've been granted the gift of revelation. The Order's agents who had infiltrated these groups throughout the years, pointed at him as one of the most influential personalities in the underground realm. He was mostly known for the announcement he made years ago: in a vision, it was revealed to him, the exact day when this Prophet will be found. Five days ago, he declared, to his congregation, that the Prophet had finally arrived.

'How long have we known this?' Asked the one with ice-blue eyes.

'For about fourtyeight hours'. Replied the one pulling out another cigar.

Aesma Daeva sat back and swung halfway in his plush leather chair. He stared at bookshelves, on the right side of the office. His narrowed eyes scanned the hundreds of titles as his mind spoke, in an ancestral voice.

'The ancient Scriptures from the Clansmen announce the impending decline of the one-God reign right as the nations of the world begin to unite. In the same chapter, they also announce the coming of who would be the last of the Prophets, the one who shall speak the New Word, in order to save, not people, but the one-God himself. This Prophet shall have as his only objective, the renewal of the idea of God, and if his Word shall spread beyond his

land, the Illuminated Ones shall see themselves, as they saw before, scattered with fear through the lands of the one-God. On the other hand, If he should fail, the idea of the one-God shall be, for thousands of years, eradicated from the hearts and thoughts of mankind, thus, leaving an unobstructed path towards knowledge'.

This knowledge was forwarded to him as a child, by the elder leaders of the past. Aesma Daeva knew this, and the one who sat across him, knew it as well, that is why the order had been giving to search, find and kill this Prophet.

'Do we know who he is?' He asked with his gaze still fixed at the books.

'Not yet, but we will soon'. Replied the other, puffing on his cigar. 'A gathering has been announced to "Celebrate The New Word" as they call it, perhaps this "Prophet" will be there'.

'When will this gathering be?'

'Tomorrow morning'.

It looked and felt later than it was, and the office became shrouded in silence and thought; only the rain outside could have barely been heard, but only because it was visible through the large windows behind him. Both were flipping through reports and photographs of their files. Aesma Daeva took another look at Lara Walker's new file, and reread her latest movements. There was a photograph of her coming out of the restaurant, after the meeting with Francis Green; she was wearing dark sunglasses, a blue office suit and heels, and carried a slim briefcase, all in all, she resembled a young professional woman, if it wasn't for that blonde spiked hair.

'When is Ms. Walker supposed to let us know about her assignment?' Asked him raising his head and swinging back to face Baphomet.

He also raised his head from his file and calculated with a frown. 'The girl *should have* traced Mr. Moone by now' He nodded as if he was trying to convince himself. 'If she have, then the Target should be down no later than tomorrow'.

Aesma Daeva tapped his fingers on the wooden desk, pondering. The city behind him grey and wet.

'And once it is confirmed that Mr. Moone *is* dead, what happens to the girl then?' He asked with mischief in his voice and void in his eyes.

The other re-lighted his neglected cigar and breathed out, long and loud. 'What happens to the girl then?' He looked at his cigar from up close, turning it with two fingers in front of his face. 'Then, she'll be put to sleep, that's it'. And blew at it slowly, endlessly, feeding its crimson tip, making it bloom in fire. Then, a voice through the intercom announced the time of the day and the next meeting of the evening.

About the Author

Gino Gianoli lives in Miami Beach, with his dog Stoli and his Apple Powerbook.

Printed in the United States
17468LVS00001B/334